# GHOSTS
# From Ch

By Michael McCarty &
Connie Corcoran Wilson

Introduction by Sean Leary

© Michael McCarty & Connie Corcoran Wilson 2008

All rights reserved. No part of this book may be reproduced or transmitted in any form or by any means, electronic or mechanical, including photocopying, recording or by any informational storage or retrieval system, except by a reviewer who may quote brief passages in a review to be printed in a magazine, newspaper or website-without permission in writing from the publisher.

# TABLE OF CONTENTS

| | | |
|---|---|---|
| **INTRODUCTION** by Sean Leary ................................. | | 5 |
| **PREFACE** ................................................................ | | 11 |
| **Chapter One:** | Resurrection Mary........................ | 13 |
| **Chapter Two:** | The Singing Ghost of Joliet Prison......... | 25 |
| **Chapter Three:** | The Shoveling Skeleton of East St. Louis. | 29 |
| **Chapter Four:** | The Whal Masion Curse.................... | 33 |
| **Chapter Five:** | Rachel and David............................ | 49 |
| **Chapter Six:** | The Hornet Spook Light.................... | 65 |
| **Chapter Seven:** | The Ghost Girl of Howard Litch Park.... | 69 |
| **Chapter Eight:** | The Ghost of Carson's Café................. | 83 |
| **Chapter Nine:** | Haunted Hallow.............................. | 85 |
| **Chapter Ten:** | The Haunted Guitar......................... | 91 |
| **Chapter Eleven:** | The Ghost Dog................................ | 97 |
| **Chapter Twelve:** | The Haunted Tractor of Jericho........... | 101 |
| **Chapter Thirteen:** | The Mystery Man of El Reno............... | 103 |
| **Chapter Fourteen:** | The Old Priest of the Rest Haven Motel.. | 113 |
| **Chapter Fifteen:** | Effie, We Hardly Knew Ye.................. | 119 |
| **About the Author:** | .................................................... | 139 |

## INTRODUCTION
By Sean Leary

A dark evening.

A wavering bonfire.

A shock of campers, huddled around the warmth, secretly seeking solace from strange noises in the forest beyond and the sounds of even odder tales being bandied about within their company.

A night of ghost stories.

Everyone has heard the sagas spun at one time or another. Some have even experienced a twist into the paranormal. And most everyone is fascinated or thrilled by the eerie appeal of the unknown.

Authors Michael McCarty and Connie Corcoran Wilson have captured this taste for the terrible and terrific in their latest book, *Ghosts Of Route 66, From Chicago Through Oklahoma.*

For many readers, some of the stories may be old favorites revisited. Personally, having grown up in the Chicago area, I remember hearing more than a few around campfires when I was a kid. "Resurrection Mary" and "The Singing Ghost of Joliet Prison" caused a few nightmares skulking around my kindergarten-aged brain and elicit smiles years later.

However, just as many, if not more, of these spine-tinglers may be new narrative ground unearthed. "The Hornet Spook Light" and "The Haunted Tractor of Jericho" were fresh treasures to my eyes -- and may be to yours as well.

At any rate, if you're a fan of ghost stories, you're certain to enjoy these offerings from two seasoned raconteurs.

Pass the book around the campfire under a starry summer sky.

Read it huddled under the blankets as the midnight wind howls outside your window.

Just make sure you leave a nightlight on afterwards.

That is, if you believe in ghosts...

Enjoy your trek through the macabre.

Sean Leary is the author of *Exorcising Ghosts, Your Favorite Band* and *Every Number Is Lucky To Someone*

www.seanleary.com
www.myveronaproductions.com
www.dingobi.com

*Ghosts Of Route 66, From Chicago Through Okalahoma* covers Illinois, Missouri, Kansas, Okalahoma and all haunted places in between. For those of you brave enough to travel this road, who saw or heard things inexplicable by normal means, "Be wary of things that go bump in the night!"

Dedication:

Michael would like to thank:

Bruce Carlson, Dad and Wilma, Mom and Doug, Steve and Amanda and Linda and Breanna, Cathy and David and Robbie, Scott and Linda and Anna, Shadow Scott, Terrie Leigh Relf, Dave and Julie Thompson, Mark McLaughlin, Ron Stewart, Camilla, Carma, The Amazing Kreskin, Dave Miller, Jim McFarlene, Dominick Salemi and "Brutarian Quarterly," The Source Bookstore, Donn Albright, The Rock Island Library, Judy Comeau and "Creature Feature Tombkeeper," Pitch Black, Scott Morschhauser, Sean Leary, Connie Wilson for co-writing this book with me and Cindy Hulting for driving with me down many dark paths on the way.

Connie would like to thank:

Bruce Carlson, for including her (long) ghost stories; "Whim's Place Flash Fiction" for selecting her short story "Amazing Andy, the Wonder Chicken" as a winner in their recent contest and "The Tabard Inn" for publishing her story "Hell to Pay" in Issue Number III (March, 2008). Also, thanks to Dr. Barbara Croft of the University of Chicago and Karen Burgess of O'Fallon, Missouri, for proofing duties. Thanks, also, to the other members of the University of Chicago Intensive Short Story Writing class who workshopped Connie's stories in June, 2007: Seth Eisner, Kathleen Naureckas, Mary Dean Cason, Phil Anderson, Diane Gillette, Michael Votta, Diane Cochamiro, Kaylea Hascall, Jacqueline Moehling, Sangetta Sinha, Patrick Thomas and Dennis Shapiro. Gratitude, also, to co-author Michael McCarty and to Connie's husband, Craig, for letting her write ghost stories in Chicago at her Writer's Lair all of June, 2007.

# PREFACE

By Bruce Carlson & Michael McCarty

"Get your kicks on Route 66"
Bobby Troup

*Ghosts Of Route 66, From Chicago Through Okalahoma* is written as if the reader were driving down Route 66, starting at the beginning of the road in Chicago, Illinois, and going through Oklahoma. Along the way, dear reader, you'll hear ghost stories about some towns on the route.

Route 66 spans eight states: Illinois, Missouri, Kansas City, Oklahoma, Texas, New Mexico, Arizona and California. It stretches over 2,000 miles of American highway and land. Born in 1926, the road gained national attention with the Bobby Troup song "Get Your Kicks On Route 66" (the song was covered by many people over the years including Nat 'King Cole). The road garnered even more attention with the 1960s television series "Route 66" which featured the characters Todd and Buzz looking for adventure as they traveled towards their destination on Route 66.

In 1985, Route 66 was decertified; it was no longer an official US Highway, but the road is far from forgotten. It is kept alive by nostalgia, fan clubs, magazines, internet websites, books ... even books like this one.

However, Route 66 is more than a road. It is an American icon, emblematic of everything from Chicago and its skyscrapers, to the Ozarks in Missouri, and encompassing grassy plains and mountains, ending in Los

Angeles, the City of Angels. It also is a road of nightmares with plenty of ghostly tales involving this highway.

The events described in this volume cover the period from the 1930s to the present. The ghost tales are not in chronological order. They are in geographical order, as though you were starting your drive on Route 66 in Chicago and ending up in Oklahoma. A second book will cover the n Texas to California portion of Route 66.

Whenever possible, diligent efforts were made to confirm these stories by gathering information from several sources and, in some cases, visiting the towns themselves. Of course, truly definitive proof was not always possible. Ghost stories are apocryphal, and some people just don't want to believe in ghosts, while others swear that they have encountered spirits in their lifetime.

The reader must appreciate the fact that, with very few exceptions such as the well known legends like Resurrection Mary and The Wahl Mansion, these stories are previously unpublished, although knowledge of the ghosts themselves may have been passed down by local storytellers. Some of these stories could cause embarrassment to people still living. Because of that, some of these stories employ fictitious names. In those cases, it should be understood that any similarity between those names and actual people, living, dead, or of the spirit world, is purely coincidental.

Both authors hope this book will serve to preserve some of the tales handed down by the locals verbally before the stories are lost to the public. These tales are part of the heritage of Route 66; they deserve to be preserved for generations to come.

It is emphasized that these are folk tales, but, also good stories. If you are looking for sensational tales of blood and gore, you won't find them here. If you are looking for stories with heavy religious or New Age content, you'll need to keep looking.

If you're looking for some interesting, informative—and, yes, educational --- accounts of the ghosts of Route 66, we invite you to spend a few hours reading *Ghosts Of Route 66, From Chicago Through Oklahoma*. Fasten your seat belts! Watch out for the thing lurking in the shadows. You're in for a thought-provoking and scary ride!

*Chicago, Illinois is the Eastern terminus of Route 66. This is where we start our journey westward traveling over 300 miles of road in the Land of Lincoln, through the Windy City, roaming on into the suburbs, and encountering one of the most famous ghosts at our first stop in Justice, Illinois...*

## Chapter One:
## Resurrection Mary

By Michael McCarty & Connie Corcoran Wilson

**Justice, Illinois**

The ghostly tale of Resurrection Mary begins with the death of a young girl or around the 1930s, some stories say it occurred on 1927. Mary was supposedly killed in an automobile accident in 1934 on her way home from the The Old Ballroom, now known as the Willowbrook Ballroom.

Some said Mary had an argument with her boyfriend, left the ballroom, and was hitchhiking home when a passing automobile hit and killed her.

Reports of the sighting of a young blonde girl, dressed in a white dress and walking along Archer Avenue began spreading in 1939, years after her death. Motorists complained that the girl dressed in a white ballroom gown and still wearing her dancing shoes, tried to jump on the running boards of their cars, or that a blonde girl dressed all in white, appeared in the road, attempting to hitchhike to the The Old Ballroom.

Resurrection Mary refused to play dead. Instead, she sought to dance the night away in the company of strangers. Many who claim to have met her never even suspected that Mary was anything but a living being. Her description by the ballroom dancers with whom she supposedly danced was always the same: a quiet blonde with icy cold skin. One man, Jerry Palus, claimed to his dying day that he danced with Mary "all night long" at the old Liberty Grove and Hall Ballroom on 47$^{th}$ Street, in the Brighton Park area. Jerry was believed to be the first living person to encounter the ghost of Resurrection Mary.

Many times, after an evening at the The Old Ballroom, the ghostly Mary would ask for a ride home, telling the driver to head north on Archer Avenue. She would converse with the drivers during the drive; the motorists were unaware they were talking to a dead girl. When Mary reached the confines of Resurrection Cemetery, she simply disappeared. Sometimes, the wraith-like girl would get out of the car, run across the road and dematerialize at the gates of the burial grounds. Once, she was spotted inside the cemetery.

A man was passing the graveyard late at night when he happened to glance towards the locked gates. A waif-like young woman in a white dress peered back at him through the iron bars. He thought she must have gotten accidentally locked in the cemetery after dark and proceeded to phone the police to rescue her. By the time the authorities arrived, the girl was gone. The policeman's spotlight shone on the iron bars to reveal that they had been spread apart. Directly at the curve of each bar, the outlines of two feminine handprints were seared into the metal bars. The bars were quickly replaced; the city claimed that the repair was needed because a truck had backed into the metal bars, but photographs of the ghostly fingerprints remained as evidence of Mary's escape from her resting place.

Reports of Resurrection Mary sightings increased after renovations to the cemetery in the mid-1970s. Although Mary has been picked up in several suburban locales, her destination is always Resurrection Cemetery.

Resurrection Cemetery is one of the largest cemeteries in the Chicago area, with more than 130,000 gravesites spread across a dark, forbidding area covering four square miles. Rather than small conventional square or rectangular headstones, the graves there are marked by many tall ornamental statues, which, at night, almost give the appearance of people trapped inside the cemetery's wrought iron gates.

Across from Resurrection cemetery is Chet's Melody Lounge at 7400 Archer Avenue, in Summit Argo (or Justice), Illinois. Chet's is a hotspot for Resurrection Mary-watchers. The bartender there, Tony Zaleski, offered a number of fascinating stories about the phantom, past and present.

I journeyed out to Chet's Melody Lounge on Archer Drive, accompanied by one friend, and spoke with the gruff-voiced bartender of six years, Tony Zaleski. First, I had called Tony on the phone; when I heard no noise in the background, I asked, "Is this a bar or a private residence?" I thought I must have the wrong number.

The voice on the other end of the line was very distinctive, a whiskey baritone. Tony was very friendly and accommodating, considering I thought I had dialed a wrong number and disturbed him. "No, this is Chet's Melody Lounge, all right," he said. "We just don't have much business tonight." It was, after all, a Wednesday night (June 20, 2007).

"Do you know anything about a ghost called 'Resurrection Mary'?" I asked.

"Of course I do," said the bartender. "Come on out after six tomorrow night when I'm working, and I'll tell you all about her. But you really should try to read some of Ursula's stuff, too." (Ursula turned out to be Ursula Bielski, who has written extensively about Resurrection Mary and other ghosts of Chicago).

At ten o'clock at night on Thursday, June 21, 2007, a girlfriend and I made the trek from Chicago to talk with Tony Zaleski, bartender for the past six years at Chet's Melody Lounge. We almost missed the spot, as it was dark and we were gawking at the creepy cemetery directly across the street. The bar, itself, is small and unprepossessing in appearance. It's a little bit run-down-looking, but friendly, in a white clapboard spooky way.

After my friend and I had settled ourselves onto bar stools in front of the long mirror that backs the bar, with three open-mouthed fish mounted at eye level staring back at us blankly, I started the conversation.

"Tony," I asked, "do you think this bar is haunted?"

Tony laughed and said, "Just last night Sarah, one of our more level-headed employees, saw a young man in a flannel shirt in the back room there, where the pool table is." Tony beckoned to a room that is separate from the front bar room where we were sitting and approximately ten yards towards the back of the structure. "Only problem is, we'd been locked up for hours and only the two of us were left inside. Plus, I didn't see a thing, but Sarah swore he was there." Tony arched his eyebrow and continued, while mixing a Bloody Mary to leave on the bar for Mary, something he and the other bartenders routinely do every night. "Yeah...a lot of my friends have felt someone tap them on the shoulder when they were the only person in the bar. They turn around: nothing. Or someone behind them will ruffle their collar and they feel a chill. Yup, this place definitely has a history." Tony poured me a glass of white zinfandel as he made this comment and shook his head up and down.

"Do you believe that the ghost of someone named Mary roams up and down Archer Drive, asking for rides?" I asked.

"Well," said Tony, with a mischievous gleam in his eye, "I'm not the one you should be asking. You should be talking to Ursula Bielski who runs the Haunted Chicago tours. Ursula met her right in this very bar when she was just a child of five."

"Really? How?"

"Mary was sitting right on that very same bar stool you're sitting on now, drinking a Shirley Temple," said Tony. I quickly moved to the next barstool before continuing with my questions.

"Why would Mary be drinking a Shirley Temple? Wasn't she old enough to drink something like this legally?" When I said "this", I held up my glass of the house white zinfandel.

Tony paused for a moment and continued, "Well, best as I remember Ursula's theory, Resurrection Mary wasn't really named Mary, at all. Her real name was Anna Norkus. Anna was a second-generation Eastern European American Chicagoan…Lithuanian or Polish, I think. The young girl was so devoted to the Virgin Mary that she took the name Marija (Mary) as her middle name. Her real first name was also not Anna; Anna was the American version of her Lithuanian name, Ona. Anna was born in Cicero in 1914. In that day and age, it was not the custom to christen infants with two names.

After 1918, children were baptized with a Christian name and a historic name, to foster pride in the person's country of origin. Anna began using the name Marija, which is Mary to us, as her middle name. She was blonde and slim and loved to dance. Some of the other candidates, like Mary Miskowsi of Bridgeport, who was killed crossing the street in late October in the 1930s on her way to a Holloween party, don't fit the physical description of the ghost that people see along this road out here." Tony indicated Archer Driver, with a wave of his hand towards the plate glass window in the front of the bar.

Also, one other Mary who was considered a candidate to be the ghost was killed about the same time on Halsted Street when she was thrown through the windshield of a car and hit an el support. That doesn't fit the profile: wrong place, wrong physical description, wrong girl. Frank

Andrejasich of Summit, Illinois, did a lot of research on the different candidates who've been mentioned over the years. From all accounts, including the color of the dress Anna Norkus was buried in (another who was thought to be the original Mary was buried in a lavender dress, not a white one), Anna Norkus was probably Resurrection Mary."

"Why does she roam Archer Drive, trying to get back to Resurrection Cemetery?" I asked.

"First things first. Don't you want to know how she died?"

"Of course. Please tell me." I was embarrassed that I hadn't let Tony finish this part of the story, first.

Tony continued. "Claire and Mark Rudnicki were former St. Joseph parishioners. They told Andrejasich that the story involving a young Polish girl of the 1940s who crashed near Resurrection Cemetery around 1:20 a.m. after she took the family car to visit her boyfriend in Willow Springs was bogus. The legend for that candidate said she had been buried in a term grave at Resurrection, but, if her family had enough money to own a car in the 1940s, why would they need to bury their daughter in a term grave?"

"I don't know, " I answered. "I'm not sure I even know what a 'term grave' is."

"A temporary one. Sometimes there would be strikes by gravediggers, and the bodies would be transferred to a term grave until the strike was over. In those days, refrigeration was not so hot, and the bodies had to be buried temporarily, until the men returned to work."

"Actually, " I said, trying for a little humor, "the refrigeration of that day *was so* hot."

I smiled, and Tony laughed and said, "Do you want some peanuts while we talk?"

A big bowl of peanuts, shells still on, materialized in front of us, and the fish mounted on both sides of the dark mirror watched us devour them, open-mouthed with envy. A yellow-gold patina bathed the room in what conjured, for me, 'instant old." We continued our conversation about Anna Norkus.

"So, Anna loved to dance and she loved life and music; she wheedled and cajoled her father, August Sr., into take her dancing for her thirteenth birthday. On the evening of July 20$^{th}$, 1927, father and daughter set out from their home at 5421 S. Neva for the famous The Old Ballroom. August's friend, William Johnson, and Johnson's date accompanied them. While driving home, at approximately 1:30 a.m., they passed Resurrection Cemetery via Archer Avenue, turning east on 71$^{st}$ Street and then north on Harlem to 67$^{th}$ Street. Unfortunately, the Chicago Street Department had left a huge twenty-five foot-deep railroad cut unmarked at that point. You couldn't see it. The car careened and dropped into the unexpected hazard, and Anna was killed instantly. Her father, however, lived; some even told him that Anna's death was God's punishment for allowing his daughter to go dancing at such a young age." Here, Tony stopped and shook his head back and forth. " It wasn't August's fault, though. Why, the very next night, there was another death at the very same place…a young boy named Adam Levinsky. So Anna's father wasn't to blame. Between July 28$^{th}$ and September 29$^{th}$ an inquest was held at Sobiesk's mortuary in Argo, headed up by the Deputy Coroner, and the Deputy Coroner agreed. The death was ruled a tragic accident.

Anna's funeral was scheduled for the following Friday. In the funeral procession were her older sister, Sophie, followed by her older brother, August, Jr. The pastor, altar boys, and a four-piece brass band preceded the casket, which was carried on a flatbed wagon with pallbearers on either side. This grim parade marched three blocks to the doors of St. Joseph's in Summit, where Anna had made her First Communion only one year before. Between the band and the priest walked Frank Andreajasich's cousin, a terrified Mary Nagode, who was a friend of Anna's in life. She had been pressed into service as wreath-bearer, in the tradition of Lithuanian and Polish funerals. Although the small friend of Anna's was terrified, her mother, Mrs. Nagode, told her that the refusal of such a request, coming, as it did, directly from Anna's father, would be a sin against Roman Catholic moral living. So, even though she was scared to death, little Mary helped lead the funeral cortege of her friend in life, Anna Norkus, to what was supposed to be Anna's final resting place, one of three newly-purchased family plots at St. Casimir Cemetery. But here's the thing," When Tony said this, he leaned in close and fixed me with a steely stare. "Anna didn't get buried in the family plot that day, because the gravediggers were on strike. Her body was transported, instead, to Resurrection Cemetery for temporary interment. Al Churas, Jr., brother-in-law to Mary Nagode, was in charge of the gravediggers and lived across from the cemetery in a house provided for him there as part of his pay. According to Al Churas, Jr., there was a strike ongoing at the time Anna was to be buried. But they had to get the girl in the ground, even if only temporarily.

So, Anna was laid to rest in a temporary grave at Resurrection Cemetery, just until the strike ended and the body could be permanently interred in the family plots at St. Casimir Cemetery. But the strike dragged on. Identifying a body later that has been temporarily buried in the heat of July in Chicago in 1927…well, let's just say that it could get ugly. So, Ursula Bielski and Al Churas, Jr., head of the gravediggers at that time, and Frank Andrejasich of Summit, who has researched the subject extensively, believe that Mary's body could not be identified when they dug her up after the strike was over. So Anna, or Resurrection Mary as she has come to be known, roams Archer Avenue trying to find her true and proper resting place. Although she always asks passers-by take her to Resurrection Cemetery, in reality that was *not* supposed to be her final resting place."

"So the theory is that she's a restless spirit in search of her true final resting place...the family plot at St. Casimir's Cemetery?" I asked.

"Something like that," Tony said, in his sandpaper voice, mopping up the bar near where we had spilled peanut shells. "Resurrection Mary is an unearthed corpse spending a restless eternity trying to find her way home."

"What other stories can you tell me that might have occurred here at the bar, regarding Mary...err, Anna?" I asked Tony.

Tony thought a moment, chuckled, and then continued. "In 1973, an angry cab driver charged into the lounge. He demanded, in a loud voice, 'Where's the blonde?'

We told him there was no blonde in the joint, but he insisted she'd just come through the door. He was looking for a young woman in a white dress who had disappeared from the back of his cab without paying her fare. Everybody here searched the place, including the ladies' restroom, but no blonde in a white dress was in the bar that night. Sometimes, people will run into the place claiming they've just hit a woman in a white dress with their car. When they get out to investigate, there's no body." Tony shrugged and lifted the bar top to lead me to a jukebox in the corner of the bar's first darkly lit room. "See there?" he said. He indicated the song ' The Ballad of Resurrection Mary' on the juke box. "Do you want me to crank that up?" asked the jovial Tony.

"No, that's ok," I said. It was close to midnight and neither my companion nor I had had any dinner. The place was beginning to creep us out, to be honest. We got directions, instead, to an open-all-night World's Famous Burrito restaurant, a few miles down the road on the corner.

    As the two of us departed, Tony called out, "Remember! If you see a young blonde wearing all white hitchhiking near the cemetery, don't pick her up!" He laughed and set the Bloody Mary he had just mixed on the sill near the front of the bar, where it sits ready for Mary's ghostly visits. The drink's been waiting for her for the past seventy years. Then, almost as an afterthought, Tony added, "But if you *do* pick her up, bring her on in here to Chet's Melody Lounge. She's run up one hell of a bar tab over the past seventy years!"

# Chapter Two:
# THE SINGING GHOST OF JOLIET PRISON

By Michael McCarty

**Joliet State Prison, Joliet Illinois**

This story took place during the summer of the Great Depression in 1932 at the old Joliet Prison on Edgehill Street (not to be confused with the more modern Illinois State Penitentiary at Joliet.) The prison was built during the mid 1800s. Its limestone walls and turrets made it one of the most secure maximum-security facilities in the country, and it housed some notorious villains. On the prison's land a deep limestone quarry and a potters' field cemetery were located, where the corpses of unclaimed prisoners who died while incarcerated were buried.

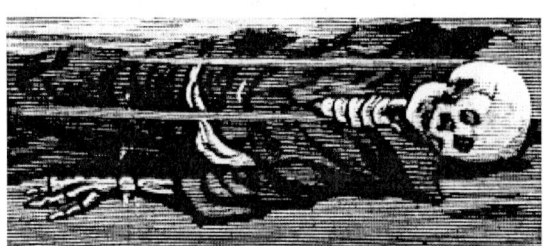

On July 16th, 1932 a local woman heard singing coming from her back yard. It was shortly before midnight and she heard a beautiful baritone singing what sounded like a Latin hymn. The lady and her daughter took a flashlight to find the exact spot, but they were unsuccessful in their search. All they knew was that the singing was coming from potter's field.

News spread that there was a singing ghost in the penitentiary's graveyard. The town newspaper, *The Joliet Spectator*, ran a story about the singing ghost. Soon, people from all over Will County and the Chicago suburbs were coming from miles around to hear the ghost singing from beyond the grave.

Thousands of people drove to the field late at night to hear the singing ghost perform. The crows got so bad that, eventually, the authorities had a Catholic priest perform an exorcism at potter's field.

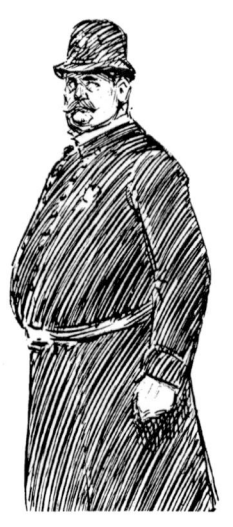

Eventually the singing ghost stopped singing.

The *Joliet Evening Herald*, in its July 29th, 1932, edition, stated the singing specter of Potter's field was an Irish-German prisoner who was scheduled for parole in early August of that year. The convict confessed to singing Lithuanian folk songs in English in the depths of the quarry. Prison officials said that the quarry made a perfect sounding board, enhancing the inmate's voice so that it was heard throughout the cemetery.

The prison official's explanation raised more questions than it answered. The location the warden claimed the singing was coming from was a quarter mile from where the voice had been heard. Stone doesn't enhance sound; it absorbs it.

Whatever the official explanation, the Singing Ghost of Joliet Prison sings no more.

# Chapter Three:

# THE SHOVELING SKELETON OF EAST ST. LOUIS

By Michael McCarty

### East St. Louis, Illinois

On a cold April evening in 1916, the residents of a row house in East St. Louis heard unusual noises coming from their backyard. In the common area behind the dwellings that served all the tenants, witnesses heard a continuous digging sound throughout the night.

When neighbors looked out their windows, they saw a skeleton, gleaming white in the moonlight. The skeleton was digging hole after hole.

When the tenants came out of their houses to investigate this eerie apparition, the skeleton vanished into thin air. The specter left behind only a number of shallow holes and, next to each hole, a tidy pile of dirt. The people of the row houses refilled the pits, but periodically the shoveling skeleton would return to dig more holes.

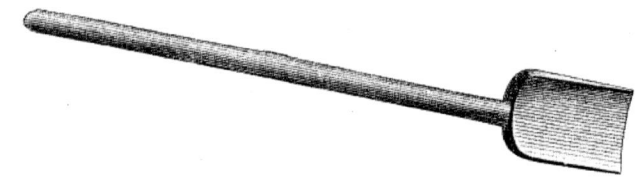

One morning just before dawn a neighbor heard his dog named Rex barking and growling. He went to the backyard. The neighbor found his pet German shepherd attacking the shoveling skeleton in his back yard. The skeleton jumped over a fence to escape. The dog dug under the fence in pursuit. The neighbor investigated, but saw no sign of skeleton or dog in the yard. Both had disappeared neither was ever seen again.

Over the course of the next thirteen months, the skeleton would reappear to commence digging once again, but only after the moon had risen in the sky. The neighbors were certain the skeleton was looking for something of value. Eventually, the neighbors began to dig up the yard themselves in search of buried treasure or lost gold.

Nothing of value was unearthed, and the residents eventually gave up their futile quest.

    The ghost of the shoveling skeleton was witnessed intermittently over the next century, but only after dark, when the sun had sunk in the west and the moon was high above on the horizon.

*As we leave East St. Louis, we cross the mighty Mississippi River and enter the Show Me State of Missouri, home of Mark Twain, the St. Louis Cardinals and the Ozarks. As we enter St. Louis, Gateway to the West, we see the Gateway Arch. We have another 300 miles of road to go. Road warriors, our first stop is at a haunted mansion. The faint of heart should remember the warning, "Abandon hope, all ye who enter here."*

## Chapter Four:
## THE WAHL MANSION CURSE

By Connie Corcoran Wilson

### St. Louis, Missouri

The wicker basket containing Charles Wahl's ashes was elusive. The ground of the remote rural acreage gave no sign of its presence, and the gravedigger seemed stumped. It was a sunny May afternoon in 1980. A smattering of relatives was in attendance at the disinterment of the earthly remains of Charles Wahl.

Among those assembled were Betsy and Charlie, great niece and great nephew of the eccentric Charles Wahl, who had died and been buried on May 10, 1949, thirty-one years earlier. Charles had spent his career in banking and finance, unlike the rest of the Wahl family, a family that made its fortune brewing beer.

Johann Adam Wahl of Eschwege, Germany, started building the family fortune in1838, with a small grocery store at Delmer and 6$^{th}$ Street in St. Louis. The light lager he introduced to the city was a great hit, and a brewery was built in 1840 near what is now the Gateway Arch. The limestone cave system at the corner of Cherokee and Hill Street, used for lagering the beer in icy refrigeration, helped Wahl's Western Brewing Company win first place amongst beers at the 1858 St. Louis World's Fair.

When Johann died, on August 25, 1862, he was a millionaire, and his son, William, would begin a major expansion of the brewery, purchasing five blocks on Cherokee, above the ice-filled limestone caves. In 1864, a new plant was built at Cherokee Street and Carondolet Avenue, covering five city blocks. By the 1870s, the Wahl family was riding high on the success of its product. Jacob Feickert, William Wahl's father-in-law, built a Victorian showcase home in 1868, the Wahl Mansion, near the Wahl brewery. The tunnel beneath the mansion, from the basement to the brewery, was only one very strange facet of the place.

"Was this really Great Uncle Charles' farm?" Betsy, the young Wahl niece, asked of her older brother Charles, also known as Charlie. She was sixteen and Charlie twenty as they gazed about at the wooded grounds of their great uncle's remote rural estate on this May afternoon in 1980, thirty-one years to the day since their Great Uncle had been buried here. Giant oak and elm trees towered above them. Flower gardens nearby wafted heady floral fragrances their way. All attention was focused on a man with a shovel in the foreground who was digging a hole. The family was loosely clustered around the gravedigger, as he attempted to locate the last known resting place of their Great Uncle Charles Wahl's ashes.

Young Charlie answered, "That's the weird part. Nobody really knows where Uncle Charles' farm *was*. We're out here today trying to find him …if he's even here. The family wants to transfer his earthly remains to the family crypts at Bellefontaine Cemetery, where all the rest of the Wahls are buried. I sure hope they find that wicker basket soon. It's getting hot out here, and I'm getting hungry." Young Charles took out a handkerchief and mopped his sweaty brow, before continuing. "Old Charles was a bit of an odd duck. He didn't do things quite like the rest of the family. Wasn't even ever in the beer business like the rest of them. He kicked around in that house like Howard Hughes or somebody for a long time. After he shot himself, Old Charles left explicit instructions that he be cremated and buried in a wicker basket on his estate. Wouldn't let the family post a death notice or wash his body or clean him up in any way, even if they wanted to. Weird."

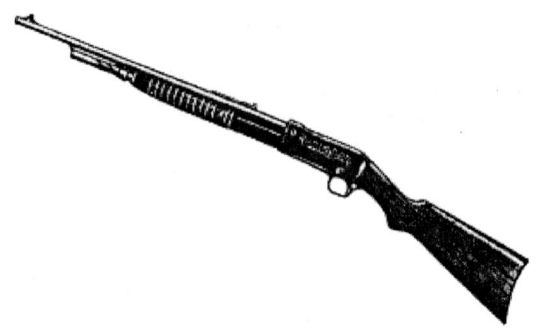

The family felt it's time Old Charles joined the Wahl party in the Bellefontaine Cemetery. But Charles, bless his eccentric little heart, wanted to be out here in a wicker basket on some godforsaken farm for eternity, buried like somebody's pet poodle. Let's just hope they find him. Fast. Otherwise, he's gonna' be pissed and I'm gonna' be pissed!" Charlie grinned his lopsided grin at Betsy. Betsy could never remain stern with Charlie when he smiled at her like that.

Betsy smiled back at her brother. She had not really known Great Uncle Charles at all. From what she did know, he was one odd duck. He was phobic about germs and wore rubber gloves all the time, for one thing.

"At least Great Uncle Charles had the good sense to leave a signed note before he committed suicide. None of the others left a note," said Betsy.

"What did the note say?" Charles IV did not know this gory detail.

"It said, 'In case I am found dead, blame it on no one but me,'" said Betsy.

"Well, duh," Charlie said. "Sounds like something one of the Three Stooges would say. Did he punctuate it correctly?"

"What do you mean?"

"You know: put a comma after the word 'dead'?"

"Oh, Charlie!" Betsy hit him on the sleeve of his seersucker jacket with her white glove. "Just because you're a writer, you don't have to be so persnickety about punctuation. It was a suicide note, for crying out loud! He had a lot on his mind when he wrote it. In fact, it was dated the day *before* he killed himself, so he must have been thinking of killing himself for at least twenty-four hours."

Betsy continued. "Well, he was found dead, all right. Just like Will and Elsa and William. Four from the same family. You *did* know that four of our relatives killed themselves, right?"

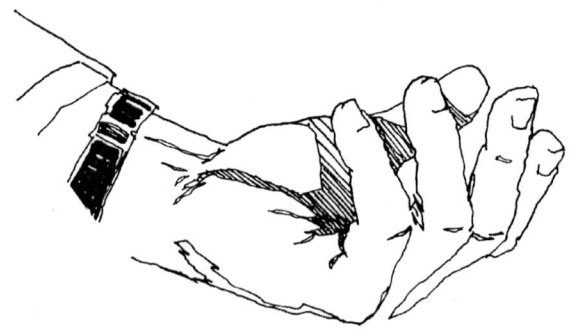

Charles seemed shocked. "No! Four? What? When?"

"You see? That's what happens when you're just too busy living out East being a writer and a playboy. You lose sight of the important hereditary nature of our family's all-consuming desire to off themselves.

Usually successfully." Betsy gave Charlie an arch look from beneath one cocked eyebrow.

Charles IV kicked at a clod of dirt as the sweating gravedigger continued his excavation, the shovel making a horrible noise as annoying as fingernails on a chalkboard. The assembled crowd all fervently hoped that the hired muscle would find the last resting place of Great Uncle Charles quickly.

"How did they all die?" Charlie was wide-eyed with interest. "I mean…I know that they killed themselves, but how?"

"Well, Great Uncle Charles here shot himself with a 38 Caliber Army Colt revolver. He was found in bed clutching the gun and, of course, he left the note. He had lived alone in that creepy old mansion at 3333 Elmer Place, with just two servants, for years."

"It might be a creepy old mansion to you, Betsy, but it was a grand place in its day. They used to have an entire auditorium beneath the place that stretched under the street and allowed actual plays to be put on by traveling Chautauqua troupes. They rigged up sets and lights and the whole nine yards. And a swimming pool! That place had a swimming pool beneath it. Imagine! Your own private underground swimming pool with water heated by the brewery's boiler house. Wouldn't that be grand? To have your own private underground swimming pool way back in the 1860s?" Charlie, lost in contemplation, seemed cheered by the thought.

Betsy was less cheerful. She was sweating so profusely that her new white dress was ruined. She continued, "There used to be a spiral staircase to get to all that stuff. It ran twenty-two feet down to the theater from the intersection of Cherokee and DeMenel, but they took it out and sealed it up, to prevent access. Mostly, Prohibition did the Wahls in."

"But," said Charlie, "people were killing themselves long before Prohibition made life tough for people who sold beer. Look at Frederick Wahl, William's son. He died when he was only twenty-eight, in 1901."

"Yes, he died young," said Betsy, "but at least he didn't shoot himself in the head like the rest of the family. He just died of heart failure. Overwork, they said. You do realize, big brother, that Frederick's death at such a young age left his father William totally devastated and was a contributing factor in his eventual suicide? William withdrew from the world. In fact, that tunnel system that you think would have been so much fun was William's way of getting to work from then on. Walked to work below ground. William just couldn't stand it when his son died. Frederick was the one who was supposed to take over the business, and then he up and died."

"Yes, but, at least he died of *natural* causes," said Charles IV.

"There's nothing natural about the way our relatives die off in droves. William finally offed himself on February 13, 1904, right after breakfast. Told the servants he didn't feel well, took a .38 caliber Smith & Wesson revolver, and shot himself in the head."

Young Charles mimicked a gun being put to his temple and the trigger being pulled. Betsy shook her head in disgust.

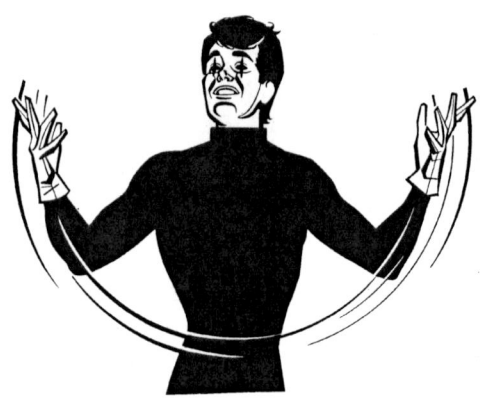

"That's just so sad, Charles. You shouldn't make fun. What a sad, sad family we have."

"You've got THAT right," said young Charlie. "William, Jr., didn't fare much better. He married the Lavender Lady."

"Who's the Lavender Lady?" Betsy really did not know as much as she was *pretending* to know about her family's past.

"Her name was Lillian Handlin. Bill, Jr., married her in 1899. From that point on, Bill and Lillian seemed to have a race to see which one of them could run through the family money the fastest! Lillian always wore lavender, so they called her 'the Lavender Lady.' She was quite the arm candy, but Bill couldn't take her spendthrift ways, so he divorced her a couple of years later, creating a huge scandal in the city gossip columns. People claim that they see the ghost of the Lavender Lady in the Wahl Mansion, you know."

"No, really?" Betsy seemed awed by this piece of information.

"Oh, yeah. The whole place is as haunted as hell! Doors lock themselves and then unlock themselves. There are cold places. People feel as though they're being watched. And then, of course, there were the rest of the deaths."

"What rest of the deaths?" Betsy parroted.

"You really don't know that much, do you?" Charles laughed at Betsy's apparent ignorance in the face of her know-it-all attitude as he said this.

"Well, Mother didn't think we should dwell on the bad stuff," answered Betsy. She sounded defensive.

Charlie began his lecture. "You know about Franklin, dead at twenty-eight, of, as you put it, 'natural causes.' Then his father, William, blew his brains out. Then there was Elsa."

"Aunt Elsa?"

"Who else?

"I always thought Elsa's husband murdered her. That's what Mom said once."

Charlie shook his head up and down affirmatively. "Well, you do have a point, little girl. Some people did think that her March 20, 1920, death was a bit strange. She and the hubby had been having some marital difficulties. Then, they got back together. Shortly after that: BANG!" Betsy jumped as Charlie, once again, did the imaginary gun to temple thing and provided the appropriate sound effect.

"It's a good thing that the digging is over and we're far enough away from that basket hole so that nobody heard that, Charlie," laughed Betsy. "You really need to have more respect for the dead. And for the family."

"Oh, I have all the respect in the world for this bunch of loons. But, as for Mom's theory that Elsa was murdered, Mom does have a point. The loving husband didn't notify the authorities that Elsa had taken a bullet to the brain for two hours. Strange, don't you think?"

"What did he give as his reason for the delay?" Betsy was processing this information.

"The usual: I was upset. I wasn't thinking straight, blah, blah, blah."

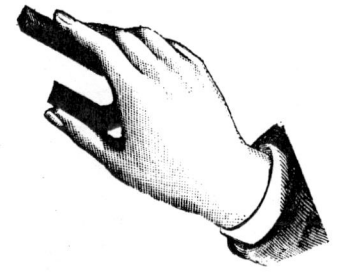

"So, Aunt Elsa might have been murdered?"

"Well, the brothers didn't seem to think so. When Will and Edwin, her brothers, showed up at the house and were told that Elsa had shot herself in the head, Will just said, 'That's the Wahl family for you!"

Charlie made a funny matter-of-fact Laurel & Hardy gesture, as though to say, "Another fine mess you've got me into." Betsy couldn't help but laugh, even though she was cross with Charles for making light of the family's tragic history.

"So, then, let me see if I have this right. First, Frederick dies young. Then, his dad William shoots himself in the head. Then, Elsa. Who else? You said four. That's only two that actually committed suicide," Betsy crossed her arms across her chest, as though she had just won an argument.

"After the 1920 shooting of Elsa, which, as you have pointed out, Mom thinks may have been a murder committed by Elsa's estranged husband, the next to bite the bullet was Will, Jr, on December 29, 1922, about two years after Elsa shuffled off these mortal coils." When Charlie used the term "bite the bullet," the pun was intentional, and he mimicked biting a bullet. "Will, Jr., talked to his wife on the phone from his office. Then, he shot himself in the heart with a .38 caliber revolver, right through his best shirt. And here's another gory detail for you. His funeral was held right in the Mansion, in his office, on December 31, 1922, two days later. But Will is interred in the Bellefontaine Cemetery in the crypt right above his sister, Elsa. You might say that they have bunk beds there. As for wives, those Wahl boys sure knew how to pick 'em."

"Stop, Charlie! That's too grim!" As she said this, Betsy laughed in spite of herself. "So, after Will, Jr., only Great Uncle Charles, he of the wicker basket, counts as one of our esteemed ancestors who ate their gun?" In spite of herself, Betsy was amused. Charlie could always make her laugh.

'The brewery was worth $7 million before Prohibition. Guess how much Will sold it for in 1911?"

"I dunno'," Betsy said, "Three million?"

"Not even close, Betsy Baby. $588,000. But Will's mom had died of cancer in 1906. She was sick with it since 1905, and Will was just not playing with a full deck at that point in time. If you ask me, this family didn't need beer; it needed Lithium or one of those other bi-polar drugs. AND a good attorney! And then, of course, Prohibition came, and the Depression. The times sure didn't help. But these family geniuses sold the brewery to the International Shoe Company for about one-fourteenth of its real value." Charles almost sounded like he was going to start making the old-fashioned "tsk tsk" noise.

"So…did anybody in this family ever die of natural causes? Besides Frederick, I mean?" Betsy asked this with a look that was both hopeful and horror-struck.

"Well, there was Edwin. He died in 1970 at age ninety of natural causes. But he insisted that all his paintings and all papers related to the family be burned when he died. Terrible thing. There was irreplaceable historical value to some of those documents." Charlie sighed and shook his head.

"Who owns the Wahl Mansion now, Charlie?"

"Guy named Paul Jones. It was a boarding house for a while, but he runs it as a restaurant/bar/hotel. It's spooky as hell in there, too. In the seventies, they renovated it, and half the workers left the job because of all the weird shit that went down while they were working. Noises. Tools disappearing. Just weird stuff."

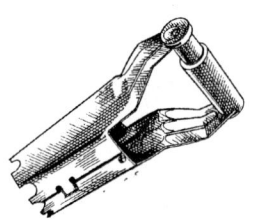

Charles, seeing that an ancient soiled wicker basket was finally in possession of the gravedigger, took Betsy's elbow to escort her back to their car. "If you go there for dinner or stay overnight, you're likely to hear ghostly knocks, phantom footsteps. Hell! The glasses in the bar have been known to fly right off the bar with nobody near 'em. The piano in the bar plays by itself. And it's NOT a player piano. Did you see last month's issue of 'Life' magazine?"

"No, why?" asked Betsy.

"You should really try to keep up, Betsy. The Wahl Mansion was named one of the ten most haunted places in the United States by *Life* magazine. That's our family's legacy."

"Really?" Betsy asked.

"Really," said Charlie.

"No wonder Mom would never let me visit the place, "said Betsy. "I don't even know where it is."

"You take Broadway from Interstate 55 and follow that to Cherokee Street. Go west on Cherokee and turn right on to Hill Street. Address is 13322 Hill Street. Wanna' go have dinner there right now?"

Betsy shot him a furtive glance and said, "No, thanks. Maybe another time."

Charlie just laughed as they slid across the leather seats of his Buick convertible.

"Okay. No Wahl Mansion food, then. Let's go find some of those St. Louis ribs that I'm always hearing about back East."

Charles Wahl, IV, started the car and Charles and Betsy drove slowly down the tree-lined lane, their attention turning from death to life.

## Chapter Five:
## RACHEL AND DAVID

By Connie Corcoran Wilson

**Webster Groves, Missouri**

When Mike and I moved into the old house at 2334 South Gore Street, between North Rock Hill Road and West Kirkham Avenue in Webster Groves, Missouri, we were intrigued by the handsome stone structure, the Rock House, our next-door neighbor.

"Wow! Look at that!" Mike's awe at the sight of this National Historic Landmark was evident in his voice. It was a great-looking place. The building had housed the Edgewood Children's Center for emotionally disturbed children next door to us since 1944.

"It's a beautiful old place, isn't it?" I said, as we carried boxes from our U-Haul to the shabby-chic old house we had just rented as our new home. The landlord had seemed very glad to rent the place to us. We found out why when we settled in and discovered the extent of the renovation that was going to be necessary to make it livable. Faulty plumbing. Creaking floorboards. Old furnace. The full complement of troubles.

"It's a good thing our rent's so low, or I'd consider moving to a fancier neighborhood." Mike was smiling. He hugged me hard, too, and patted my pregnant stomach. I knew he was just having fun with me. We both loved the large leafy oak trees of Webster Groves and the grand houses that stood all around us. Ours might be a bit more run-down than the rest, but we were moving up in the world, for sure.

"Awwww! Don't be like that. This is a terrific neighborhood. Why, the trees around here have to be at least one hundred and fifty years old! I read somewhere that a lot of this area was built around the time of the World's Fair in St. Louis. Don't you think this street looks just like that Judy Garland movie?"

"What Judy Garland movie?"

"You know…the one where she sang 'Clang! Clang! Clang went the trolley!'" I sang the verse, to get Mike's full attention, just as he was plugging in a standing lamp, only to discover that the electricity to the outlet seemed to be non-functioning, as well.

"Oh! That's 'Meet Me In St. Louis.'"

"Louie?" I asked, with a laugh. Mike came over and hugged me tight once again.

"You better not be meeting anybody named Louie. You're my wife, and I'm very happy that you are." He kissed me softly on the cheek and returned to the lamp.

"Just think, Meg. It's our very own home. Our first house."

"RENTED house," I reminded him with a grin, just to keep things real.

We were newlyweds, married just shy of a year. Up until now, we had been living in cramped apartment quarters. One place we had lived, we even had to go down the hall to use the community bathroom, so "our very own place," as Mike had dubbed the run-down two-story frame house seemed palatial to us. We were ready, willing and able to start a family. I was four months pregnant, but I wasn't showing, yet. This would be a great house for a child. Mike had just been appointed regional manager of the new chain shoe store down the road at the mall. Life was looking up.

The chill in the late October air made the fireplace inviting, but a small disaster with the flue left us banging on the ancient radiators. We prayed the heat would kick in before we turned to popsicles. We were having trouble making anything work in the decrepit old house.

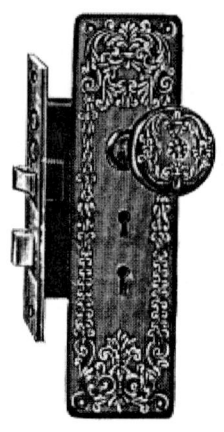

"Let's huddle together for warmth," Mike said, laughing.

"You just want an excuse to huddle. I'm not sure it's for warmth." I hugged him in return. "And we both know where that impulse has gotten us." Just then, our attention was caught by a red-headed boy of about twelve approaching our house from the direction of next door's Children's Center.

"Straighten up and fly right, Boy-Oh. Wouldn't do to terrorize the neighbors. Especially since they're all supposed to be children with emotional issues." The doorbell rang.

A ruddy-faced carrot-topped boy of about twelve stood there on the porch when I opened the door, clipboard and pen in his hand. Behind him, clutching a toy stuffed unicorn and silently regarding us with big blue eyes was a little girl who looked about six, presumably his younger sister.

"Hello, Mrs." he said, in a courtly old-fashioned manner. "Would you care to order a Christmas wreath from the Edgewood Children's Center? It's not much money. We'll deliver the wreath to you a month before Christmas. We're just taking orders now."

He looked so eager to please and was so polite that Mike and I both said, in unison, "How much?"

"Only $10. They're real. Blue spruce. It'll smell great, and it'll look great on the front door of this fine house." He smiled. Apparently the redheaded entrepreneur was not above a little insincere flattery. Anything for a sale.

"What's your name?" we asked simultaneously.

"David." He shuffled from foot to foot, the cold wind making his ruddy cheeks appear rosier.

"You cold, David?" I asked.

"Yes, Ma'am."

"Want to come just inside the door while I give you our information? And maybe you'd like a cookie? We have some Oreos in the kitchen somewhere." Mike and I were addicted to Oreos, always arguing about eating them "the proper way." We had made sure before we packed the kitchen stuff in our former apartment that the Oreos would be right on top, so that we could have a quick pick-me-up of sugar whenever we wished. And, of course, we could also have our favorite debate over the "proper' way to eat an Oreo, with me favoring the white filling first and the cookie last, and Mike the reverse. We joked that we were like Jack Spratt and his Mrs. from the famous nursery rhyme.

"I'd like a cookie, Ma'am, but what's an Oreo?" asked the shy, polite boy, as he stepped inside.

"You've never heard of Oreo cookies?"

"Oh! So it's a type of cookie, then?"

"Why, yes. Yes, it is." I didn't know anyone who wouldn't recognize the brand name.

"What about your little sister?" I asked David. The girl was lingering on the sidewalk. She had not climbed even one step up towards the top step of the porch stoop.

"Oh, Rachel won't come in. She don't talk."

"Can she have an Oreo?" I asked. In this day and age, you had to be careful about handing out candy or cookies to strange children.

"Sure. But she won't say please and thank you, proper-like. It's just her way. She don't talk. And she won't come inside, either. She got scared real bad. After that, she just quit talking." I wanted to ask what had scared the poor thing that badly, but I didn't want to pry into personal matters.

"That's okay. If she can stand the cold, we'll give her an Oreo to eat outside while she waits for you. It won't take but a minute to give you our information. Her pet unicorn can have one, too." As I said this, I extended two Oreo cookies towards the silent girl with the gigantic blue liquid pools, staring at me, clutching the pink stuffed unicorn as though it could save her.

Rachel took the first cookie and held it to the stuffed unicorn's pink mouth. The unicorn did not take a bite. No surprise there. Rachel held the second cookie in her hand, her fingers clutched tight around it. She made no move to put the Oreo in her mouth. Silence.

"Well, Rachel. We'll have your brother back in a flash. Feed that unicorn while you wait." I smiled in what I hoped was a kindly fashion as I shut the door against the cold. I could see that Rachel had not moved even one foot from the spot on the sidewalk she had chosen. She grasped the Oreos firmly in her slender fingers.

"Our address is 2334 South Gore Street, David, but we don't have our phone hooked up, yet. We're the Hansens....Mike and Meg Hansen."

"Oh, that's okay, Mrs. Hansen. We'll deliver the wreaths personal-like, but not till one month before Christmas. I'll collect the $10 then."

"That sounds fine, David. And don't forget your cookie!" David turned to leave as I almost forgot to give the young salesman his reward. I remarked, "It wouldn't do to give your sister Rachel TWO cookies and not give you even one!"

"It's okay, Mrs. Hanson. Rachel won't mind. She knows I'd do anything for her. She'd share her cookies with me, if you forgot." And then he was gone, giving us a last sad lingering look over his shoulder. He walked down the three steps to the porch and rejoined his waiting sister and her pet unicorn. He took Rachel by the hand. They walked toward the cottonwood tree in the backyard of the Edgewood Children's Center, fading into the haze of swirling smoke from autumn bonfires in the neighborhood of huge trees.

*Pyrite benzine*, I thought to myself as the children disappeared in the haze from the burning leaves. *Nasty stuff. That stuff can kill you. Those kids shouldn't play near that bonfire. The people who work at the Home should keep them away from that smoke. I hope the kids don't have asthma.*

In the two weeks that followed, we learned more about the history of the Edgewood Children's Center, researching it on the Internet. The children's home was over one hundred and seventy-five years old. Originally, the St. Louis Association of Ladies had established it for the Relief of Orphan Children after the cholera epidemic of 1832. In 1834, the ladies came to the aid of the poor orphans, founding the Center. By 1848, the place had been renamed the Saint Louis Protestant Orphans' Asylum. The asylum wasn't located next door to us on Gore Street, then, though. It had only moved to the Rock House, as it was known, in 1869. The Reverend Artemus Bullard, a preacher, operated a seminary for young men in the Rock House next door until he was tragically killed in a train wreck in 1855.

Reverend Bullard was a strong believer in the abolition of slavery. The Rock House was one of the stops on the Underground Railroad, helping runaway slaves. A tunnel several blocks long ran beneath the Rock House. Slaves from the South routinely hid there on their way North to freedom. In 1890, two children became lost in the tunnel and died, though. After that, the exit was sealed off.

In 1910 a fire gutted the Old Rock House. The interior was destroyed, but the lovely stone exterior remained just as we saw it daily through our kitchen window. A six-year-old girl perished in the blaze that year, although her older brother tried to save her and died in the conflagration himself.

As we continued to unpack our few belongings, following David and Rachel's departure, a middle-aged lady wearing a plaid Burberry muffler picked up our package of paper plates. Dislodged from the kitchen goods, the package of plates had taken flight in the strong gusty winds of the late October afternoon chill. They behaved almost like a giant pack of Frisbees.

"Here you go," she said, with a laugh, as she placed the plain white paper plate package she had retrieved from the street into my chilly hands.

"Thanks so much," I said. "I was afraid I was going to have to break out my track shoes to catch those things… and who knows where they are?" I laughed. "That wind is really fierce." I hoped my smile conveyed my genuine gratitude at the friendly gesture from the stranger, the first adult we had met.

"Not a bit," she said, extending her hand. "I'm Lucinda Resnick. I was just getting off my shift at the Center. I stay through the nights on Mondays, Wednesdays and Fridays. But, since it's Thursday, I get to go home and actually cook and care for my own family."

"You have children at home?" I asked. My question came more from curiosity than politeness. I wondered how the woman could manage to stay overnight next door while supervising active children of her own at home.

"Oh, yes. My husband is a fireman. He works weird shifts that we can usually coordinate. You know…week on, week off stuff. I really love kids. Including my own, " she said, laughing. "These kids need me more even than my own, though, because most of them have emotional problems. Different traumas, you know. It didn't start out that way, of course. The home originally was for orphans from the 1832 cholera epidemic, but, over the years, and with the move here to Rock House, today's kids all seem to have psychological problems. You know the drill. Kid comes home and finds his father hanging in the basement. Parents leave to play golf and Mom and Dad never come home, killed in a car accident. Eventually, those kids wind up here." She said all this so matter-of-factly that I was impressed with her efficient, calm demeanor.

"Well, it's wonderful work that you do, " I said. And I meant it. "We met the young red-headed boy, David, and his sister, Rachel, just an hour or so ago. They seem like such nice, polite young people. Although it's sad that Rachel doesn't speak. Why is that? Do you know?" I had been wondering about the small, frail six-year-old with the big blue eyes and the pink stuffed unicorn pet, clutching her Oreo cookies and waiting for her older brother. Wondering why Rachel didn't speak. What unspeakable horror had her deep blue eyes seen?

Lucinda seemed startled. "David? When did you meet David?"

I turned to Mike for confirmation. "It takes an hour, right?" I asked Mike. He was hammering away at something on the front porch, two nails in his mouth. Mike just nodded assent.

"Yes, one hour ago David came selling Christmas wreaths. Reasonably priced ones, too. We ordered one and gave him a cookie. His sister, Rachel, wouldn't come inside, although we gave her an Oreo, too. David said she doesn't speak. He was such a courtly young gentleman. Very Old World. So polite and courteous." I smiled at Lucinda, expecting her to smile in response. Instead, she wore a puzzled expression, so I went on. "I don't think I've ever met a child or an adult who didn't know what an Oreo was, though. I had to explain to him that an Oreo is a cookie."

"How old was this David?" she asked.

"About twelve. Why?"

"We have a David at the Center…the only one…," Lucinda explained, "but our David is six feet two with dark hair. David Leibovitz. He's Jewish. He wouldn't be selling Christmas wreaths."

"What about Rachel?" I asked. "Do you have a Rachel? Little girl of six. Big blue eyes?"

"Yes and no," Lucinda finally said, with great reluctance.

"What do you mean? You do have a Rachel? A small six-year old who won't speak? Or you don't have a small girl with big blue eyes who just stares at you as though she's clairvoyant or something." I had noticed the unusual nature of Rachel's stare. I felt uneasy under her gaze, as her friendlier older brother chatted to us about the wreath.

"There was a young girl named Rachel in the home many years ago. She had an older brother named David. Both were orphaned by the flu epidemic, and so they came to live at Edgewood. Near Christmas in 1910, the house caught fire. Rachel was trapped in an upstairs bedroom. David died trying to rescue her. Sometimes, people say they can still see a red glow in the upstairs bedroom on the right. That was Rachel's room. There are residents who claim to have seen Rachel swinging in the swing in the old cottonwood tree. Others say she floats in the air near there, especially at Holloween. Of course, you can't believe kids when it's Holloween, now, can you?"

"Did Rachel have a pink stuffed animal…a unicorn?"

"How did you know?" Lucinda asked. She opened her car door, preparing to leave.

"I saw them both. Remember?"

Lucinda quickly slammed the door to her car shut without comment. She started the car and drove away, no longer our friendly new neighbor, but a spooked white-clad nurse from the institution next door who probably thought we were both nuts.

Mike finished nailing the loose porch boards. We both just stood there, absorbing everything we had just heard.

"Do you remember that neither one of them ate the Oreos?" I asked. "In fact, David didn't even know what an Oreo was!"

"Well, to be fair, the unicorn didn't eat the Oreo, either," Mike said, his eyes signaling a joke.

"The unicorn is a mythical beast, Mike." I sounded cross. I was really just struggling to understand the unknowable. I was spooked.

"My point, exactly, " said Mike, as he opened the door to our home at 2334 South Gore Street, and we returned to reality. "Guess we should just plan on picking up a wreath ourselves when we get our tree," he added with a crooked smile.

"Funny. Very funny."

I moved to the computer and quickly googled "Oreo" cookies. 1912. Oreo cookies weren't invented until 1912. The fire that killed both children occurred in 1910.

We hugged each other and moved to the couch in front of the fireplace, as a chill pervaded the room.

"Mike?" I asked.

"Yeah." He settled deeper into the comfy chintz couch.

"When we have the baby, if it's a boy, let's name it David."

Mike looked at me seriously. His eyes wrinkled with understanding. "And if it's a girl?"

"Rachel, of course."

The fire crackled in the fireplace, warming the cold room, and I almost could swear that I smelled the crisp aroma of blue spruce.

## Chapter Six:
## THE HORNET SPOOK LIGHT

By Michael McCarty

**Joplin, Missouri**

Twelve miles southwest of Joplin, Missouri near the Missouri-Oklahoma line, in the Ozark foothills, strange light bounces in the dark sky: the Hornet Spook Light has been a paranormal enigma for over one hundred years.

The strange light appears in the tri-state region of Missouri, Kansas and Oklahoma. The lights have been called the Ghost Lights of The Ozarks, the Joplin Spook Light, the Tri-State Spook Light, the Indian Light, the Neosho Spook Light and the Devil's Jack-o-Lantern.

Best observed from ten o'clock at night until dawn breaks, the orange lights have been known to enter cars and buses. One light even chased a vehicle down the road and caused the car to catch fire. This ball of fire has been spotted by area residents hovering over their gardens, shining outside their bedroom windows, floating above the treetops and bouncing on their porches.

Indians along the infamous Trail of Tears first saw the haunted orb in 1836; however, the first official report occurred in 1881 in a publication called "The Ozark Spook Light."

E40 or E50 have both been called Spook Light Road. At the intersection of E50 and State Line Road stands the Spook Light Free Museum, built by photographer Arthur Posie Meadows. However, somewhat fittingly, the museum was destroyed by fire in the 1980s.

The US Army Corps of Engineers studied the Spook Lights in 1942, but no one has been able to provide a conclusive answer as to their origin.

Folklore about the light says that Indians attacked a miner's cabin while he was absent. Upon his return, he found his wife and children missing. The miner is said to be searching for them along the old road, using his miner's lamp.

One resident said this of the light, "There used to be an old bar near Spook Light Road where my dad would take us when company visited from out of town. We kids loved to go there, play pool and listen to the old man who owned the bar tell stories about the light. Often we would sit outside on the car to watch for the spook light. We had to be real quiet, or it wouldn't come out. As we watched, all of a sudden it would appear at the other end of the road. My dad would leave his lights out and try to creep up on it. When we got near the light, it would suddenly burst like a bubble and then re-appear behind us."

*As we leave the Show Me State, we cut the corner through Kansas, one of the shortest parts of Route 66. There are only thirteen miles of the old road here. Click your heels like Dorothy and get ready to travel the familiar road into the Sunflower State...*

## Chapter Seven:
## THE GHOST GIRL OF HOWARD "PAPPY" LITCH PARK

By Connie Corcoran Wilson & Michael McCarty

**Howard "Pappy" Litch Park
Galena, Kansas**

It is June, 2003, in Galena, Kansas, and the Galena Good Old Days celebration is in full swing in the newly-dedicated Howard "Pappy" Litch Park. The park is named for Howard "Pappy" Litch, a local historian and beloved citizen of Galena, Kansas. The land for Litch Park was once a federal weighing station, but Darrell Ray of Joplin, Missouri, worked tirelessly to establish a memorial to the Will Rogers Highway (also known as Route 66), on this very land.

"I think that we should try to preserve as much of the spirit of the good old days of Route 66 as we can," Darrell said in a newspaper interview documenting the many monuments he helped establish up and down Route 66. Mr. Ray spent his life on projects devoted to memorializing the highway popularized in both the television series of the same name and the Nat "King" Cole song. In a sad foreshadowing of what would happen during Galena's June, 2003, *Good Old Days* celebration, Darrell Ray died of a heart attack the Thursday before he was supposed to be present at the celebration of the Mother Road in Litch Park.

The celebration went on without Darrell Ray, or, for that matter, without Howard "Pappy" Litch, who had been dead for years when the park was dedicated to him. Galena residents flocked to the site to dedicate the green, grassy area. Judy McCanns Morris even had a dream of reviving her parents' drive-in, the Dairy Dream, for one day. Judy's plans to revive Darell and Naydene McCanns' good time gathering spot of the fifties and sixties did not come to pass on this sunny June day, but her dream lives on. She still hopes to restore the Dairy Dream to the "in" status it enjoyed as a gathering spot in Galena, Kansas, during the fifties and sixties.

What was happening at Litch Park this day, however, was music and lots of it. Various bands had set up on stages in the park. Street musicians like Kenny Keene were welcome, too, and Kenny had brought his slide guitar to entertain the crowd.

Three children---Hannah, Emma and Jack---sat wordlessly on the grass in Litch Park, entranced by the music. The oldest child, Hannah, a girl of eight clad in pink shorts, played with her pigtails. The pigtails had matching pink bows, pretty against Hannah's flaxen hair and angelic face. Hannah's sister, Emma, two years younger, was wide-eyed and quiet, awed by the music and the crowd and the trees above. The littlest child, their younger brother Jack, diaper-clad, sucked on a pacifier, waving a toy tractor like a dangerous gunslinger, as though, at any moment, he might gouge out his own eye or that of one of his sisters. Jack wore a floppy sun hat that made him appear absurd, like a cartoon character. At the very least, he was a concussion waiting to happen. Little Jack stomped his right foot on each downbeat as the slide guitar man played louder and the music grew more frantic.

"Jack, sit down!" Hannah commanded the boy as though she were his mother. Mom and Dad were divorced. This was Dad's weekend to entertain the kids.

"Oooog!" From Jack, that was high praise. Jack had not yet begun to speak in sentences, and, with his penchant for sucking on a pacifier, he might not say anything intelligible for a long time.

The brown-hatted street performer, intent, concentrated on the intricate fingerwork, his mouth working in a weird warped way.

The musician said, "I wrote this next one at a kitchen table in Independence, Kansas," and sang, "The sky above me brings me down…"

The weather in the new Howard "Pappy" Litch Park this day was beautiful, balmy and eighty-four degrees. The musician delivered the refrain perched on a bar stool in the shade of a canopy of "Y"-shaped grasshopper-green trees on this brilliant spring day. A battery atop a large wagon powered the microphone that carried his original melodies to two hundred attentive listeners arrayed in a ragged semi-circle. He was a street musician, and a good one.

It was the divorced dad's day to entertain his children. The father seated his brood of three in a row, down front.

"Hannah, take Emma's arm. Jack, come back here." Dad was having trouble corralling the active boy, but once Hannah, the eldest, sat down, Emma and Jack also sank to the grass. Jack was already on his feet again, stomping his right foot along with the bass-line of the song.

"Why do I have to sit next to Jack?" Emma asked. She knew the answer. Nobody would really be sitting next to Jack, as Jack would be on his feet most of the time in that always-on-the-go way little kids have.

Obedient, good kids, they followed their older sister's lead in seating themselves, although Emma pouted when Dad ignored her pleas to be placed further from young Jack. Emma tried to distance herself from Jack and Hannah throughout the day, and that helped some to explain what happened later.

The silver metallic slide guitar the man was playing enthralled Hannah. She was hypnotized by the way his fingers caressed the strings, flying across them. She stared intently at the man's rapid-fire fingers, as he worked the frets nimbly, only fifteen feet in front of her, his right sandal-clad foot tapping out the beat on a piece of wood.

Aligned in a row in yoga lotus position, the trio of children watched the musician manipulate the slide guitar. They looked as though, if they could understand this, it might reveal some secret of life. They were mesmerized. A smattering of crowd applause greeted each new riff, the next run faster than the last. The music reverberated, crescendoed.

"Thank you, ladies and gentlemen. And kids, " the singer said, nodding and smiling towards his front-row audience of three. "Anything you can donate today is appreciated. CDs are for sale to the left. Just ask the lovely Misty, who's over there holding them up. She'll be happy to sign them for you." The blue bucket rapidly filled with green bills; the tempo of the musical selections increased.

"Daddy, can we buy a CD?" Hannah asked. The line forming in front of the blonde sandal-clad Misty was long. People were hungry to take home a moment of musical magic. The black-clad father stood near his seated children, plastic beer cup in hand.

"We'll see." The generic parental non-answer for the ages.

Dad was a nondescript man of perhaps forty, six feet tall, wearing black tee shirt and black jeans. He had the athletic look of a man who had played football in his youth. A protective papa, he reached down to adjust the goofy hat his young son wore, shielding the boy from the sun's rays. He tousled Emma's hair, and she giggled.

"You like the guitar man, Kids?" he asked, between songs.

"Yes, Daddy. Can we get his CD? Can we?" Hannah was fanning the flames of consumerism on this glorious day. Soon the others would join in, trying to wear their father down.

Glancing down at the fascinated kids as they followed every riff from the accomplished musician in the battered brown hat, Dad smiled a father's proud smile.

A young couple approached. They assumed a position directly in front of the children. The young girl of the duo was perhaps eighteen, wearing hoop earrings and a gray poncho. She leaned her head against the young man's shoulder. Her boyfriend wore flannel pajamas in a wild blue plaid print. A white tee shirt completed his outfit. He looked warm, sweaty and uncomfortable as he played with the girl's left earring, which was as big around as her wrist. The boy's arm below the tee shirt's cuff bore a barbed wire tattoo. The couple was oblivious to everyone, indifferent to all stimuli but the music and their bodies, pressed together so closely that they looked as though they could melt into a giant blob under the sun's rays.

Together, merged in a romantic tableau, the teenagers formed an impenetrable barrier, obscuring the view of all those behind them in the crowd, especially the view of the three small seated children. The young couple's wishes and desires were all that mattered to them. Their view, their entertainment, their experience was paramount. Only the hypnotic beat of the singer's music interested them, and the pressure of flesh on hip, girlfriend against boyfriend, bodies leaning against each other, confirming their union, melding two into one.

The father realized that his children could no longer see the performer. He stepped forward and lightly tapped the young man on his right shoulder. Nothing. A second polite tap. Pajama boy paid no attention to the older man.

The father stepped closer to the young man's right shoulder a third time and whispered in his ear.

"Young man, could you and your date move just a few feet to the side, so that my kids can see the guitar player?" The father smiled as he asked the question. The young man gave no sign he had heard him, not even glancing at the older man. The young couple remained obstinately stationary.

The father stood there, fuming. No words were necessary to convey his anger, his frustration. His emotions were transparent, a silent movie, no sub-titles necessary. An incident was about to play out. A dark look bruised the father's furious eyes. His agitated state grew with every passing second. His body tensed like a cat preparing to spring. In a frantic burst of energy, the older man moved two to three feet ahead of the couple and placed his body directly in front of the impassive pair. He turned and said to the indifferent duo behind him, "How do you like it?"

The couple didn't respond.

The black-clad father abruptly returned to his place behind the couple, four feet in back of them, standing next to his three children. He lean forward again, towards the young man's right shoulder, took one step forward, and said, into the pajama-clad boy's right ear, "Screw you!"

The boy finally turned, slowly, to look at the unhappy man. "What did you say?"

"I said 'Screw you, you low-life. These are little kids here. They were here first. You're ruining their good time."

The father stood there, almost quivering with rage. He had tried to block the couple's view as they had blocked his children's gaze, but he was only one man. The couple neither acknowledged his remarks nor moved.

Little Jack's foot no longer stomped along with the bass-line. He no longer smiled. The children's concentration has been fragmented. The oldest girl, Hannah, now wore a look of growing concern. The children's mood of happy enjoyment has been shattered.

The children remained seated on the ground. They now looked as though they might spring to their feet and take flight. Hannah, the oldest girl, began twisting the pink ties on her pigtails faster, a gesture of worry. She squinted up at the overarching lattice-like canopy of trees above their heads. Emma, clad in a pink and orange top and blue jeans, studied her sister's upturned face tensely from a distance, trying to decipher what is happening. Her glance flitted from face to face like a darting moth. She has distanced herself a bit from her siblings, sitting three to four feet away. Little Jack began to lose interest, started to look away, and dropped his toy tractor in the dirt. Jack would cry soon. It was evident in the way he had stopped dancing.

"Well, excuuuuuuuuuse me," the boy said, in an imitation of an old "Saturday Night Live" skit line he had heard in countless re-runs. He turned his back and once again ignored the older man.

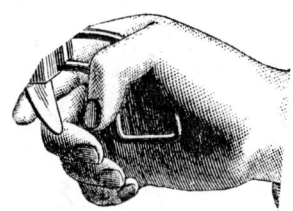

Irate, the father thrusts his hands deep into his pocket. He was almost apoplectic with rage. He pulled his right hand from his jacket pocket, the fingers wrapped around an object. Something metallic glitter on his palm, caught the sunlight. Glinted there, but could only be seen for a brief moment.

The song ended.

"We're gonna' take a little break to tune the guitars here, folks. We'll be back in a few. Thanks so much for your contributions. Any money helps keep us on the road. Please be considerate; throw us a buck. Be considerate of your fellow park people, too." The singer had noticed the developing trouble, and he had done what he could to help, while hitting up the crowd for one last donation before taking a break. And, hopefully, before real trouble started. A crowd engulfed the singer, gathering around him for autographs. The father still seethed.

The young couple finally broke their static pose. They moved down the gravel of the park's pathway, towards the rose bushes, away from the father and his three cheated children. Slowly ambling, the lovers were in no hurry.

The older man reached out to his restless children, helped them to their feet.

"Stay here just a minute, Honey," he said to Hannah, the oldest. "Watch Emma and Jack."

"But, Daddy…" Hannah started to protest, but Dad was gone, following pajama-boy and his date deeper into the park. The metallic object was just barely visible, concealed inside his left hand. The pajama-clad boy was now within two feet of the frustrated parent.

   At some point, the boy and his girlfriend nonchalantly crossed directly in front of the man, rudely cutting him off. The lovers had been strolling at a leisurely pace, unconcerned, oblivious, arms around each other's waists. The couple and the furious father approached a remote and heavily wooded area of the Howard "Pappy" Litch Park. Few of the day's celebrants where present in this area, were the bugs were out in force.

The father opened his hand, took the silver thing, placed the brass knuckles over the fingers of his right fist.

"Hey! Punk! I'm not going to excuuuuuuse you." The older man swung hard and a bright burst of red sprayed from the teenaged boy's nose.

The girlfriend screamed and jumped on the father's back. He responded by yanking at one of her giant earrings, pulling it from her ear. She collapsed in the grass, sobbing.

"Maybe you won't be such a jerk next time we're celebrating the Good Old Days." The father stood above the younger man, seemingly triumphant; the boy seemed shocked to have been attacked.

Others in the park were beginning to notice the brief violent encounter. The angry father suddenly remembered that he must return to his three children. He turned to go, but pajama boy rose from the grass and launched himself at the older man's turned back in a counter-attack.

"Okay, you two. Break it up. Come with me." The policeman interposed himself between the two struggling male forms and escorted them to another part of the park, ignoring the father's pleas.

"I've gotta' get back to my kids, Officer."

"I see. And that's why you attacked this young man unprovoked?" The officer didn't seem sympathetic; he had witnessed the first blow from across the park's green expanse, but not the lead-up to the conflict.

"No…it wasn't unprovoked. But, I can't tell you the whole story right now, I've got to get back to my kids. Come with me. I'll explain later." Dad pointed to the general area where the performer, now gone, had been singing, and where his children had been sitting.

Eventually, the officer agreed to lead the man to the general area where he said his kids waited for him. Hannah was there, holding little Jack on her lap.

"Where's Emma?" Dad asked.

Hannah looked up, terrified, red-eyed from crying. "I don't know, Daddy. She was here, but I was chasing Jack. And then she was just… gone."

Hannah whimpered a bit, all that was left of the active crying she had been engaged in for over half an hour. A crowd had gathered around the two small children, comforting the crying girl and her brother.

The father shouted to the people around Hannah. "Did anyone here see a little girl, about six, wearing a pink and orange top, blonde hair and blue eyes? Answers to the name Emma?"

A murmur ran through the crowd, as though they were reluctant to speak. Finally, one woman came to the front of the anxious group.

"I saw a woman come by and pick up a little girl dressed like that. I thought it was her mother." The stranger seemed almost apologetic, as though she were somehow to blame for not questioning the woman about her actions at the time.

"How long ago? Which way did she go?" It is the Officer who is now asking questions. He is gradually accepting the father's concerns as his own.

"I don't know how long…maybe twenty minutes? She went towards the parking lot."

Everyone rushed to the parking lot.

Dad, distraught, hugged Hannah and Jack, comforting both of them. The young man looked on, surly, nursing his bloody nose, his girlfriend holding a Kleenex to her equally bloody ear.

There was never any description of the kidnapper provided that could help the police locate the mystery woman who took little Emma during the Good Old Days celebration in Galena, Kansas. Some said the kidnapper was young and blonde. Some said she was tall and brunette. After taking testimony from the crowd, which had not realized that the woman was not Emma's mother, the descriptions were so varied as to be useless. No one saw the woman place the youngster in a vehicle. Some did say that Emma was crying, but Jack and Hannah were also crying, so Emma's tears did not seem out-of-the-ordinary. Emma was only six, after all.

Every year in the four years since the event, residents who visit Howard "Pappy" Litch Park in Galena, Kansas, report hearing a crying child when the park is deserted. They also sometimes see a small figure, clad in pink-and-orange, climbing on the playground equipment---the swings, the Jungle Gym--- near dusk, but, when the observers draw near, no child is present. At night, the strains of slide guitar music seem to waft through the Park, coming from far, far away, and, sometimes, children seem to cry along with the sad, sad music.

*We're in the last state, Oklahoma, where Route 66 has the most road of any state in the United States. In 1926 there were four hundred and sixteen mile of the old road that ran across the Sooner State; by 1937 Route 66 in Oklahoma had been reduced to three hundred and eighty-three miles. The shrinking of Route 66 in Oklahoma is but a sign of the fate the road will eventually undergo across the nation, leaving behind small towns with run-down motels and tourist attractions that have become ghost-like, themselves.*

## Chapter Eight:
## THE GHOST OF CARSON'S CAFÉ

By Michael McCarty

### White Oak, Oklahoma

They call the passage where US 69 in Afton, Oklahoma becomes Route 66 and curves "Dead Man's Curve" because the curve is a harrowing drive. But when drivers survive the ride and pass the scenic pecan groves of the Little Cabin Pecan Company, they will see the famous "Eat At The Carson's Café, Good Food Since 1945."

In the parking lot of the café, especially late at night or on a rainy evening, area residents claim the ghost of Abigail Lundeen will appear. Motorists describe the tormented specter as being a frail brunette wearing only a thin white nightgown, who wanders the parking lot, the spot where she died in an automobile accident in the winter of 1953.

According to legend, young Abigail had been recently married and was driving in the middle of the night during an ice storm. Her husband's truck had crashed on the side of the road on "Dead Man's Curve." She was on her way to pick him up that night, but her car crashed in the Carson's Café parking lot, overturning many times, killing Abigail instantly.

It has been reported that the ghost of Abigail Lundeen still wanders the parking lot by the light of the moon, beseeching drivers, "I've been in a car crash, please help me…."

Then Abigail Lundeen vanishes into thin air.

**Chapter Nine:**

**HAUNTED HOLLOW**

By Connie Corcoran Wilson

**Timber Ridge Cemetery
Cataloose, Oklahoma**

Cataloose, Oklahoma is only a small town…barely 6,000 people at the last census (5,449 in the year 2000), but it contains enough haunted places for a town ten times its size. The area has the distinction of being an inland port, linking Chelsea to the Arkansas River and, eventually, to the Gulf of Mexico.

A more benign feature of the small town is the Blue Whale that Hugh Davis put in place in a lake nearby for his wife Zelta, who collected whale figurines. This large whale/lake area eventually grew to become a campground and attracted a rather large tourist trade, when Route 66 was in its heyday. With the passage of time and the death of Hugh Davis in 1990, the Blue Whale Park built for wife Zelta fell into disrepair. While some of the Blue Whale campground has been restored in recent years through a fundraising drive, it is far from what it was when drivers got their kicks on Route 66.

Since then, the city has accumulated a sad and ghostly history. Maybe it is because the area once witnessed the historic Trail of Tears in 1834, when the Treaty of New Echota resulted in the forcible removal of the Cherokee tribe from that area to lands west of the Mississippi.

The Indian leaders did not accept the federal government's directive to move, but President Andrew ("Stonewall") Jackson sent government troops to enforce the removal of 15,000 American Cherokee Indians, 4,000 of whom died on the journey. The Indian Removal Act of 1830 set the stage, perhaps, for the more modern misery that has followed as recently as 1976, when a young girl on what is now called Karla's Bridge jumped to her death in an area known as Redbud Valley. Residents claim that, ever since her suicide, they hear laughter and see fire in the area of the bridge.

Also of relatively modern origin is the legend surrounding the suicide of a young girl at a dance at the high school. A young girl killed herself in the bathroom while at a school dance. The bathroom was located near the old gym of the high school, and that area of the school has been said to be haunted, ever since.

The strangest ghost story of all for this area located six miles east on Highway 412 is the story of the young Indian boy hit and killed by a car in 1989. The victim was riding his bike when he was struck and killed He was buried in the Timber Ridge Cemetery, an area which is also known as Haunted Hollow by local residents. The boy's grave was located in the first row of graves, next to the gate at the bottom of the hill. The very name "Catoosa" means "hill" in the Cherokee language.

Beginning in 1993, drivers started to report seeing a boy kneeling by his bike by the side of the road. Often, the drivers had to swerve to miss the young man, as they came up over a hill and encountered him suddenly.

One such person reported it this way, "As I came up over the hill near Timber Ridge Cemetery, I saw a young boy kneeling next to his bicycle. I braked, in an attempt to avoid hitting him. I drove through what appeared to be a white cloud. I heard the sound of impact and thought *Oh, my God! I've hit him!*

I immediately got out of my car to check. There was no body in the road and no sign of any body nearby, but there were bloody handprints on the fenders of my car and new damage to the front end of my brand new Impala.

I entered the cemetery itself, thinking that perhaps the impact of my car striking the child had thrown him over the fence and into the graveyard. As soon as I entered the dark and forbidding cemetery, my nose began to bleed. Shortly after this, I saw what appeared to be a fire burning at the crest of the hill, beyond the graves.

I got back in my damaged auto and drove into town with Highway 167 to the east and Highway 44 to the west of me. I found the City Hall and, because I was trying to do the right thing, entered, looking for a policeman.

A large Indian gentleman in a policeman's uniform greeted me. "Can I help you, Sir?" he said.

"I've hit a young boy with my car, but I can't find the body. I got out immediately to render assistance, but there was nothing there in the road. I came up over the hill and he was just…there. It all happened so fast!"

"Where did this happen?" asked the officer.

I explained my location, in an area that I later found out was called Haunted Hollow by the locals.

"Sir, I'll take pictures of the damage to your car, but first let me show you something."

After he said this, the officer opened the drawer of his desk, reached in and pulled out a file. He put the file on the desk, opened it, and I saw photos of at least twenty automobiles with markings and dents on them similar to what I had just seen on my own 1993 Chevy Impala.

"These cars all reported hitting something in the neighborhood of Timber Ridge Cemetery. Most of those reporting an accident thought they had hit a small boy who was kneeling by the side of the road near his bike, a boy they saw too late to avoid striking him when they came up over the crest of the hill. No body has ever been found, but we have had at least twenty such reports since 1993. As you can see, some of the drivers have had similar damage to their vehicles. Of course, I will go to the site with you and investigate, but, Sir, I doubt if we will find anything."

And, of course, the officer was right; when we later returned to the area, we found nothing.

After his last statement, the officer closed the folder, put it back in the desk drawer, and headed out to my car with me to take Polaroid pictures of the damage to my front right fender and hood and, eventually, to accompany me to the Timber Ridge Cemetery.

When the policeman had driven back into town, leaving me by the Cemetery alone, I left Cataloose driving very slowly, lost in thought. As I neared the gates of Timber Ridge Cemetery, returning the way I had come, the gate itself seemed to have taken on a life of its own, opening and closing randomly, even though no one was there.

I could not get out of Haunted Hollow and Cataloose, Oklahoma fast enough, and I will never go back.

## Chapter Ten:
## THE HAUNTED GUITAR

By Michael McCarty

**Erick, Oklahoma**

Erick, Oklahoma isn't Nashville or Memphis, but the small town has had its fair share of musical talent born there. Roger Miller was a native, famous for his song "King of the Road." Sheb Wooley, famous for the song "Purple People Eater," was also from Erick. Both singers have streets named after them in Erick, and there is a Roger Miller Museum located there.

Del Connors lived in Erick, but commuted to Oklahoma City to work for an architectural firm. On the weekends he played country music in area bands.

In 1985 while strolling through a pawnshop in Oklahoma City he found a 1966 custom cobalt blue Fender Telecaster that had painted flames running up and down its neck.

"The guitar was in excellent shape, considering that it was used," Del said. "The frets were hardly worn, I adjusted the neck, bought new strings, and the guitar sounded like it was brand new, which is remarkable for a guitar almost twenty years old."

Three weeks after Del purchased the guitar, strange things started to happen.

Del said, "I heard some loud music coming from the basement where I kept the guitar. I had a recording studio down there, so I thought maybe I might have left one of the tape recorders on. When I went downstairs, the music stopped."

He looked around the basement and saw nothing out of the ordinary.

"I was going back upstairs and I started hearing loud music. I recognized the song; it was 'Purple Haze' by Jimi Hendrix. I ran downstairs, flipped the light back on, and the music stopped. I looked at my amp; it was unplugged. It smelled like something was burning. I looked around and still didn't see anything unusual. I touched that Telecaster. It was burning hot."

In October 1986 a strange occurrence happened while Del's band was playing at a country bar. "Any time we played a song by a Top 40 country artist that was alive, the guitar wouldn't play a single note. But if we played the songs of dead artists such as Johnny Cash, Waylon Jennings, Patsy Cline, Carl Perkins or Elvis Presley, the guitar played perfectly. Very strange."

A couple of weeks later, Del was practicing songs in his basement studio and the guitar kept going out of tune. "It was very eerie. I would tune the guitar, and a few seconds later the whole guitar would go out of tune. Then I'd retune it again and it would go out of tune. I tune mostly by ear, and I have a good ear. I took out my electric tuner and it would still go out of tune but according to the tuner it was perfectly tuned."

Del changed all six guitar strings and the guitar was still out of tune.

"This was getting to be very frustrating," Del commented. "I took off those strings and put on a very expensive set of strings and the guitar was still going out of tune."

He decided to call it quits for the night when suddenly all six of the expensive strings snapped off the guitar simultaneously.

"I never saw anything like that before. I put the guitar on the stand and all the brand new strings broke off at the same time. I have been playing guitar close to fifteen years. It scared the bejesus out me."

In the summer of 1987 a power failure occurred while Del was playing with his band.

"I was starting to play a guitar solo and the bar went black. All the lights and power went out at once," he said, still spooked by the incident.

"About ten minutes later, the power came back on. My band began playing all over again and, when it came to the guitar solo, all the power went out again. This time, when the power came back on, I switched guitars."

In the fall of 1987 while he was practicing in his studio basement, weird sounds started coming from his Fender amplifier.

"I like to use my '60s amp with the guitar; they sounded great together," Del said. "But that night the amp was making a horrible noise; it sounded like bad static. So I turned off the amp. I still had my guitar plugged in, and the noise still continued, even after I turned it off. I finally unplugged it from the wall."

Two nights later, the same thing happened: bad static coming out of the amp.

Del was ready to unplug the amp, when it sounded like voices originating from the amp.

"I listened really carefully and the faint voice sounded like it said 'The night is very dark. The grave is very cold.'"

Over the next couple of years, Del played the Telecaster less and less.

In the winter of 1989, while he was playing with his band, he decided to play the Telecaster again. "We were going to do the song 'Jambalaya (On The Bayou)' by Hank Williams. The Telecaster always sounded great doing that song," Del said.

In the middle of the Hank Williams song, the guitar began getting hotter and hotter. "It felt like it was on fire," Del said. "My fingers were being burned. The strap on the guitar tore in half. I looked at it later, and saw that it had burnt off."

At the end of the night he packed the Telecaster in the back of his car and returned to the bar to get the rest of his equipment.

"When I went back to my Oldsmobile, the car was on fire. The fire was coming from inside my trunk, where I had just put my Telecaster. I ended up losing the Telecaster and my car, but I didn't have to worry about power failures during solos or having my guitar burn me when I played, after that."

## Chapter Eleven:
## THE GHOST DOG

By Michael McCarty

**Elk City, Oklahoma**

Elk City is known for two things: it is the birthplace of songwriter Jimmy Webb who penned the song "MacArthur Park" (which was a Top Forty hit for actor Richard Harris and disco diva Donna Summers) and it is the location of the National Route 66 Museum.

In 1942, a car hit Eddie Selgin's dog Midnight. "I was ten years old at the time. I loved Midnight," he said. "To have my dog killed like that was a great loss to me. It still chokes me up to think about it, after all these years."

Midnight was a black Labrador retriever with a white spot on the top of his head.

"That marking was very unusual. It is something you never forget," Eddie said.

Twenty years later in 1962, after Eddie had moved from Elk City, been married, and fathered two children, he returned to Elk City to care for his dying father. The thirty-year-old attorney had many legal matters to attend to in town.

"Everywhere I went, I saw Midnight. The dog I kept seeing was all black, with that white spot on its forehead. There was no mistaking Midnight. I called his name. He'd look at me with recognition, but then he'd run away."

Eddie saw Midnight outside the graveyard when his father was being buried. After the funeral, when Eddie had packed everything and was about ready to leave town, he saw Midnight one last time on the Timber Creek Bridge as he drove out of Elk City.

Eddie does have a theory why Midnight reappeared in his life. "It was a troubling time in my life, when my dad died. Maybe Midnight came back to help make me feel better. If Midnight was a ghost, I wasn't scared of seeing him. Seeing Midnight again made me feel better. Midnight's presence was somehow comforting."

When Eddie returned home he went to the Humane Society and adopted a black and white Cocker Spaniel for his family. The kids named it Dawn.

"I hadn't had a dog since Midnight," Eddie smiled. "I went from Midnight to Dawn, which seems only right."

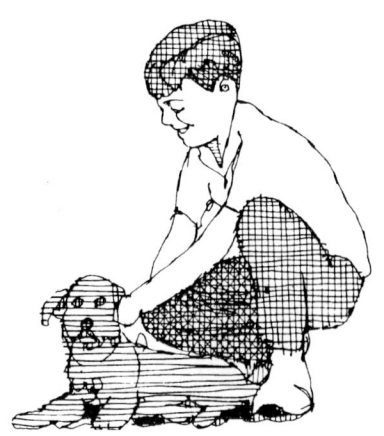

## Chapter Twelve:
## THE HAUNTED TRACTOR OF JERICHO

By Michael McCarty

**Jericho, Oklahoma**

    Brent Norman was driving his old rusty John Deere tractor on Route 66 in 1951. He loved that tractor. The seventy-year-old farmer had just finished harvesting his forty acres of corn and was taking the tractor in for repairs. While he was driving back to the house, Brent had a heart attack and died, his John Deere tractor crashing into a tree and tumbling down a steep hill, crushing Brent beneath its giant wheels.

Over the years, motorists reported seeing a rusty old tractor either on the side of the road or tumbling down a hill near Jericho. But the tractor had no driver; it was always driving itself.

"I wanted to pass the tractor," said one driver, who agreed to tell us his story on condition of anonymity. "The tractor was going so slowly that I was becoming frustrated. I kept honking, hoping it might make the driver go a little faster. Finally, I moved into the passing lane, and, when I drove past the tractor, I was shocked to see there was no one driving it."

If you see a rusty tractor around Jericho, proceed with caution.

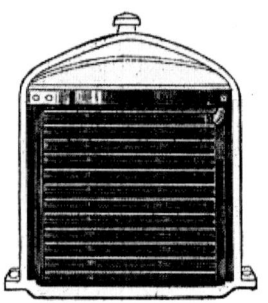

## Chapter Thirteen:
## THE MYSTERY MAN OF EL RENO

By Connie Corcoran Wilson

**El Reno, Oklahoma**

El Reno, Oklahoma is a town with 16,222 inhabitants who enjoy normal pleasures like a good hamburger. The presence of a federal prison in El Reno makes the residents feel safe and protected, as they reside at the junction of Route 66 and the Chisholm Trail, also known as I-40 and U.S. Route 81. The residents' hamburger fetish reached its peak in 2006, when El Reno won the Great American Main Street Award while cooking up an 850-pound hamburger on Fried Onion Burger Day. The twentieth celebration of that day will be in 2008 and an even larger hamburger will, no doubt, be fried in the town 25 miles west of downtown Oklahoma City.

But El Reno has a darker side...one that may be partially attributable to the number of tornadoes the town experiences, a number 306% greater than the overall United States average.

While driving through El Reno, towards Weatherford, I neared Fort Reno, which was built in 1874. Ahead of me in the road I spied an elderly gentleman wearing a brown trench coat and a brown hat like the ones Humphrey Bogart always wore in his films. I was driving a white Ford Taurus. It had been a long day on the road as a traveling computer consultant. The day had dawned bright and sunny, but fog had moved in around noon and now, at about 4 p.m., a light drizzle was spattering my windshield when I pulled abreast of the old man, who seemed to be struggling to walk up the steep incline.

I rolled down my window and something possessed me to speak to him.

"Hey, Old Timer! Do you need a ride? I'm going just up the road a bit. I could give you a lift over this hill."

The old fellow looked unkempt and disheveled. He pulled his brown fedora even lower towards his eyes, eyes that burned with an unhealthy fire as he ceased his plodding up the hill and reached for the handle of my rental car. As he slid into the front seat next to me, I tried to strike up a conversation with him.

"I'm new in these parts.... really just here to make a sales call at the Canadian Valley Technology Center out on old Route 66. I'm in computers. What do you do?"

The old man just stared at me, his eyes barely visible beneath the brim of the ridiculously old-fashioned hat. I thought perhaps he had not heard me, so I asked a different question, "Where are you going?"

When I asked the second question, the old man turned his head away from me, and seemed to stare out the side window of the car at the drizzling downpour. I decided that he must be shy, or perhaps just hard-of-hearing. Maybe he didn't even speak English.

*I'll just chat him up a bit,* I thought. *Maybe he'll come around and start responding.*

The wind had now risen to gusts that were shaking the small car as though it were a leaf about to float off one of the nearby oak trees. The wipers kept up their rhythmic "click, click, click," trying to clear the steady downpour from my windshield. In a matter of moments, the sky had turned from light afternoon gray to a dark unhealthy shade of pewter and brown, and then I saw it: a tornado funnel not one hundred yards off to my left.

"Oh my God!" I exclaimed, completely absorbed in the drama as pieces of plywood flew from the walls of the nearby reconstruction of Fort Reno. The pieces of plywood, which were at least feet five by five feet, flew into the air as though they were matchsticks. They resembled stamps as they gained altitude and were sucked towards the vortex of the funnel. I didn't know whether to stay with my vehicle and park it or make a run for the nearby Fort, which now loomed in the distance, as foreboding as a European castle. In my fear and excitement, I had completely forgotten the silent stranger riding shotgun in the front seat of my Ford Taurus, until I heard my name whispered loudly, in a voice that sounded like a death rattle.

"*Jonathan*," the voice wheezed. I glanced towards the old man in the brown weathered trench coat and the pulled-down brown fedora, but his gaze was still averted. How did the guy even know my name? I hadn't given it.

"What did you say?"

The stranger steadfastly avoided my eyes, but, again, I heard my name whispered, more loudly this time. It seemed as though it were coming from the back seat, directly behind me. Truthfully, it was as though the keeper of a crypt had whispered my name, just before the mausoleum doors closed on the casket containing my cold dead corpse.

*"Jonathan!"* Again the sound of my name reverberated in my ears. I did not know where to direct my attention. Should I keep my eye on the mysterious stranger sharing my vehicle, should I check the back seat for an unwanted and potentially dangerous intruder, or should I run from the approaching tornado?

The voice seemed to be gaining in both volume and proximity. I also thought I detected the sound of footsteps, growing nearer, approaching me from behind at a fast pace. This was impossible, as I was seated in a moving vehicle, but I had slowed to a snail's pace while mesmerized by the looming danger of the huge funnel cloud eclipsing the horizon. The sheer power and magnitude of the tornado was awe-inspiring; fear had turned my blood to ice.

Just then, I glanced to my right to see my seatmate's reaction. I was just in time to see the old man hurl himself from the moving vehicle. Luckily, I was driving only about five miles an hour at the time, my attention diverted by the danger of the approaching funnel cloud, which was now uprooting huge trees and churning a nearby body of water into three-foot high waves. It looked as though an eggbeater were whipping the small stream into ocean waves. I assumed that the fellow in my front seat was as scared as I was by the approaching storm, and had decided to take his chances in seeking shelter to avoid the storm.

But why would the old man jump from a moving car? And where had he gone? He did not seem to be on the road, nor did I see him in the ditch nearby. He seemed to have completely vanished. Why wouldn't the old man speak to me when I spoke to him?

Since the funnel cloud seemed to be turning in my direction, I had no time to search for the missing hitchhiker or ponder these questions. I had to make a run for Fort Reno; the 230 foot-long Commissary and the 1876 Officer's Quarters in the distance appeared to hold out the best hope for me to ride out the storm. Although the buildings were old, recent renovations had strengthened them, and if the Commissary had stood since 1885, chances were it would weather yet another of Oklahoma's famous tornadoes. Still, the sky had turned a sickly brownish color, which reminded me of the mysterious hitchhiker's clothing. My mouth had gone dry with fear, and I could only think of one thing: get to the protection of the walls of the Fort before the storm's full force hit.

I gunned the Taurus' engine, hoping to outrun the now 120 mile-an-hour winds. As I sped towards the gates that would give me access to the grounds of the Fort, ahead of me, bent double by the increasing winds, I saw a familiar figure. I had just traveled at least five miles going a minimum of 80 miles an hour. How could it be? How could the frail figure in the distance be the very same hitchhiker who had silently entered my car and then, so suddenly, thrown himself from it at the height of the storm just a few miles back?

I was gaining on the vagabond. Even though I could not believe it to be the same person, his dress was distinctive. I felt that it would not be right to deny a fellow human the chance to outrun the demon storm bearing down on us. After all, this fellow clad in a brown trench coat and wearing what appeared to be the same brown fedora as before pulled down over his eyes, was making very little headway in the path of the ferocious storm. He was bent almost double. Even my small car was having difficulty in the wake of the ferocious wind. Without a ride, this man stood no chance at all of making the sanctuary of the Fort's Officers' Quarters or its Commissary in time.

I rolled down the window a second time, the wind beating down on my small vehicle and carrying windswept rain, rain flying horizontally from the intense wind, directly into my face. I shouted as loudly as I could, "Get in! I'll drive you to the Fort!"

The mysterious stranger turned, fixed me with a calm gaze, as though he alone of all creatures was unaffected by the chaos turning our world upside-down. I leaned forward to open the door for the man, who was holding his trench coat shut against the force of the wind with both hands. For an instant, my gaze was averted, focusing on the door handle to open it for the elderly gentleman. When I looked up, the brown trench coat-clad man was gone, completely vanished, leaving nothing in his wake but the fedora hat that was quickly being sucked east into the vortex of the funnel.

Unable to linger, I completely floored the accelerator, desperately seeking to outrun the worst storm I have ever personally witnessed. I just cleared the gates of the Fort and hurled myself into the Commissary when the full force of the winds, later clocked at 150 miles an hour, hit the building. A falling tree had totaled my car. All the windows had blown inward, the flying glass cutting my hands and face. I cowered under a table as objects in the room flew about the room, leaving it in disarray. Later, I wondered how the building and I had survived at all.

Now, when I see footage of hurricanes hitting Miami, I am reminded of the day I ran for my life from the tornado funnel. It was also the day that I met the mysterious trench coat-clad ghost of El Reno, Oklahoma.

## Chapter Fourteen:

## THE OLD PRIEST OF THE OLD BLUE HEAVEN MOTEL

By Michael McCarty

**Blue Heaven Motel**
**Afton, Okalahoma**

"My dad said he always regretted not taking me to a buffalo ranch as a kid," the 30-year-old man told me between sips of his coffee. "My father had a business trip in California and he took Route 66. This was some time during the late 1970s. On his way back from the trip, he stopped and stayed the night in a town called Afton. The motel was called Blue Heaven. Before leaving to return home, Dad' stopped by a buffalo ranch. He'd say, 'Danny, next time we go on vacation in Okalahoma, I'm going to take you to a buffalo ranch.'"

"'You'd really love the place.' my father would say, a gleam of pride sparkling in his light green eyes. 'The place is crawling with buffalo. They have this one buffalo that does tricks. I think his name was Black Barney, but I can't remember for sure. There is a petting zoo; they have deer, elks, ducks, peacocks, yaks --- even llamas. The place has the world's largest western wear store and a barbecue joint called the Dairy Ranch. Here: I bought you a couple of postcards of a buffalo ranch.'

The first postcard showed a lake and trees. It simply read:
'Greetings From Afton, Okla.'
The second postcard was of a building that had a sign saying:
'Buffalo Ranch Trading Post' with a couple of wooden Indians standing in front of a teepee.
"On the back of the postcard was the address of a buffalo ranch," the young man said finishing up his cup of joe. "I put those postcards in my scrapbook. I used to look at them all the time, dreaming of the day I would be able to go to a buffalo ranch."
"Did you ever go there?" I asked.

"I'm getting to that," he said. "Last summer my fiancé, Mindy and I decided to spend our vacation in Los Angeles. We had a lot of vacation time left--- about a month--- so we decided to take the old Route 66 to California and, since my father always talked about the place, we'd stop by a buffalo ranch.

"It took us two days to get to Oklahoma. I had looked up the address. We didn't see any buffalo ranch, so we pulled over to a restored service station and looked at a map.

"I was studying the map, when this pick up truck pulled up next to me. This older man got out of the truck. He saw me looking at the map and asked, 'What are you looking for? I'm from Afton, maybe I can help you find what you're looking for."

"'I'm looking for a buffalo ranch," I said. "It should be around here somewhere. I'm not sure where.'

"'That's because you're at it,' the stranger said.

"'This is a buffalo ranch?' I asked, confused.

"'Used to be,' the older man said. 'The owner, Aleen Kay, died in 1999 and now the place is a service station. Afton used to be a hot spot for tourists back when Route 66 barreled through our small town, but the damn government decertified the road. Changed it from Route 66 to I-44. You don't hear people singing songs about getting their kicks on I-44. Everybody would always stop at a buffalo ranch before that. It's kind of sad. Good day,' he said, as he prepared to leave.

"I looked at Mindy and said, 'What do you want to do now?' And she said, 'I don't know, Dan. What do you want to do?'

"'Maybe we can stay at the motel my dad stayed at, the Blue Heaven. That place sounds heavenly. We can eat dinner, than get an early start tomorrow. I've been driving for hours and I'm a little tired of the open road.'

"As we drove into Afton, we found the remains of the old Blue Heaven Motel. Another disappointment. The buffalo ranch was now a service station and the motel was in ruins. The sign was so rusty that you could barely read it. Most of the letters had faded away. It would have been more appropriate if it had said 'Rust Heaven,' since it was covered in rust and corrosion.

"Mindy could see I was disappointed. She said, 'I packed some food in a cooler this morning. We have a blanket in the trunk. Let's have a picnic here.'

"We had a picnic on the grass on the side of the motel, near the building. The weather was unseasonably warm. It was starting to get dark. Mindy looked up at the motel and saw an old priest standing in front of a window, looking down at us. It creeped her out," he said.

"The priest had gray hair, dark sunken eyes, and a scar that ran across the left side of his wrinkled face. His stare was menacing."

"'There shouldn't be anybody in there,' I said, 'The place hasn't been occupied in years.'

"I told Mindy that I was going inside to investigate, but she didn't want to be left alone, so she came with me. We walked to the window and looked in at the gloomy room. There was nobody there; not a soul."

"'Here's the weird thing. The floor was extremely dusty, so if someone had walked across it, there would have to be footprints,'" He paused, casting a frightened gaze my way. "There were no footprints on the floor of that room. We left, tired or not. We drove out of Afton and never returned."

## Chapter Fifteen:
## EFFIE, WE HARDLY KNEW YE

By Connie Corcoran Wilson

### The Sherman Hotel, One Main Street
### Chelsea, Oklahoma

"Give me a shave, Effie," the patient said to the attentive nurse sponge-bathing him in his hospital bed.
"Now, Robert. You know my name's not Effie. I'm Lucy." The nurse continued washing the injured 84-year-old, who, even though he lay dying, constantly made passes at all the pretty young nurses. Lucy smiled indulgently at the old man.

"As soon as I get out of this damn-fool place, I'm gonna' take you out for a night on the town," said Robert B. Sherman, oil-rich millionaire and owner of the Sherman Hotel in Chelsea, Oklahoma. Bob coughed up blood and sputum from his lungs, which Lucy, his nurse, wiped away. Two weeks after inviting Lucy to go out dancing with him, Robert B. Sherman was dead.

Robert B. Sherman didn't take Lucy out on the town in Chelsea before he died. Shortly after that exchange with his nurse, two weeks after a stroke felled the seemingly indestructible oil millionaire, he was dead, leaving his wordly goods to be squabbled over by his three children, and leaving behind a whispered dark legacy.

Robert, a farm-implement salesman originally from Minnesota, had single-handedly created a new town in Texas, Prairie Vista, located 18 miles north of Austin, simply by showing pictures of a big red strawberry to neighbors in the frozen Midwest in the dead of winter and inviting them to come enjoy "the sunshine in Texas." R.B. made his money hitting oil in places like Spindle Gulch, and he made lots of it. But money can't buy everything, and R.B. Sherman was dead before he could take his nurse Lucy out dancing in Chelsea, or prevent the death of the love of his life, Effie.

Bob Sherman could sell anything to anyone, as proven by Prairie Vista. R.B. sold the biggest bill of goods to Effie Waterman (not her real name), a maid in his showcase hotel in downtown Chelsea, Oklahoma, located at One Main Street and Broadway. Effie was a pretty thing---a maid in the hotel less than half Robert's age. She was twenty-five when R.B. first noticed her, and he seventy-five.

"Effie.... you know I'm lonely, honey. A man has needs. My wife, Hattie's, been dead for five years now. A man has needs."

"But...R.B. Will you take care of me? I mean, after? Will you respect me and take care of me?" The pretty brunette looked fetching in her maid's uniform as she brushed a stray wisp of hair away from her oval face. She was a good girl, a devout Baptist, and she was dubious about her employer's proposition, although she had come to know Robert Sherman as a warm, gentle, caring individual.

Robert B. Sherman had been very good to her during the two years she had worked at his downtown Chelsea hotel, and he was promising to be very good to her now, if she would share her time with a man growing old alone, but not yet past the point of desiring a companion in his sometimes-lonely life.

The truism about life at the top being lonely had hit home hard for Robert Sherman these last five years, as squabbles with his three adult children, Ruby, Maggie and Robert Junior, had consumed many of his waking moments. The three children Robert had with his first wife, Evelyn, were strong-minded, stubborn individuals, just like him, especially his oldest daughter Ruby. Ruby had differing ideas about how the family's money should be invested.

When their mother Evelyn had been alive, she could always steer the troubled family's ship away from the reef of family discord, but with Evelyn dead of breast cancer now these past five years, R.B.'s oldest daughter, Ruby, had become more and more outspoken about her father's plans to expand his already grand hotel, and son, Robert Jr., always a pale imitation of his spirited father, and younger sister Maggie had let themselves be caught up in Ruby's objections to R.B.'s investment plans.

"Sure I will. Effie…you know me. Have I ever been anything but good to you? Of course, I'll take care of you!"

Having someone to love and someone who would love him in return, was Robert B. Sherman's top priority in life now. What good was all the money in the world if you had no one to share it with? He desperately wanted to convince this pretty, kind young woman to share his good fortune with him. He would build her the finest palace in the world, just to keep her by his side.

Robert B. Sherman often told friends that his hotel was going to be "the Taj Mahal" of hotels, little realizing the irony of his words. The Taj Mahal, after all, had been built as a tomb, a gravesite built by a grieving husband to memorialize his dead wife. When R.B. approached Effie of the Sherman Hotel, he did not intend to entomb her in the shrine he meant to build, but, in effect, that is what happened.

So it was that Effie Waterman (not her real name) came to be the mistress of one of the richest men in Chelsea, Oklahoma, a man who had built the grandest hotel in all of Oklahoma, a man over twice her age, and a permanent resident of the hotel that W.B.'s famous daughter, Ruby referred to as "Father's 300-room hobby."

R..B. was constantly adding floors to the hotel. When it opened in 1911, it was two 10-story towers and featured imported Austrian chandeliers in the lobby. Price tag: $10,000 per chandelier. Then Ruby---who had contributed vast amounts of Daddy's oil money to secure that her favorite candidate won the Presidency--- was named Ambassadress to Lichtenstein. Ruby began hostessing lavish Washington, D.C., parties, which also brought attention to R..B.'s masterpiece, the Sherman Hotel in Chelsea, Oklahoma.

Lavish parties in the nation's Capitol were expensive, and Ruby wanted the Sherman fortune(s) to continue to grow, so that she could cement her position there as the Hostess with the Mostest of Grand Parties given.

There was even a Broadway play written about the colorful life of the gregarious and generous Ruby Sherman, who liked to throw the family money around almost as much as her flamboyant father. It was probably inevitable that, as Ruby's stature grew in the nation's Capitol, she would clash with her equally strong-willed father.

In 1930, R.B. added more floors, until the hotel was fourteen stories high. Ruby didn't like that. "The General," as R.B. called her, wanted the money Dad used on expanding the hotel to be used, instead, to drill for more oil. More oil meant more money for more parties, in Ruby's mind. Ruby and her father had invested together in oil fields near Oklahoma City in 1930 and had discovered wells that had the potential to produce up to 40,000 barrels a day.

But now, in 1944, R.B. wanted to build another twenty-eight-story tower to add to his masterpiece, what R.B. had dubbed "the Taj Mahal of Hotels." Ruby---who knew nothing of her father's secret agenda regarding Effie--- thought this plan was just pure foolishness. She convinced her sister Maggie and her brother Robert Junior of the folly of their father's actions, as well. It was Ruby who lodged the first lawsuit to remove R.B. from managing his own affairs.

R.B. had promised to "take care" of Effie. When Effie announced that she was with child, he employed a mid-wife to deliver the child in the hotel, itself. Best to keep any breath of scandal away from friends and family. It wouldn't do to have Chelsea tattle-tales know about his mistress and their love child.

"You know I'll take good care of you and the baby, Effie. Didn't I promise to take care of you? Have the Little One and I'll put you up in the Penthouse of the hotel." R.B. beamed at his own generosity, teeth clenched tightly on his omnipresent cigar, and Effie ...who had come to really love the old man....responded with a small, grateful smile.

Effie, a chambermaid of modest means from a family of humble origins, good Baptist girl that she was, was overwhelmed at the thought of actually living full-time in the penthouse with the spectacular view, the corner suite that overlooked Main Street and Broadway. Until now, she had occupied a much-smaller room on the ground floor, a room that had housed other maids in other years as well as the occasional traveling engineer, brought in to fix the hotel's unique boilers when they malfunctioned. The first-floor hotel room was just that: a standard hotel room used by many who were traveling through the area in a transient fashion but had business with R.B. Sherman.

But the penthouse, which R.B. had had craftsman working around the clock to complete for his illicit love, was a massive room with dark mahogany wainscoting, dark wood floors, and a fantastic view of the city below. An expensive Austrian crystal chandelier, like those in the lobby, was a highlight of the multi-room Penthouse. It was not just a room; it was an entire suite, with all the modern conveniences—truly a palace fit for a King's consort.

Effie Waterman gave birth to R.B. Sherman's fourth child, a daughter, in the Penthouse, with a private mid-wife supervising. Effie and the child were now hidden from view in the 14$^{th}$-floor penthouse of R.B.'s grand hotel. Or his "grand hobby", if you cared to use the term used by his daughters.

Before, when Effie was in residence in the first floor room, she would mingle with her co-workers and, unbeknownst to R.B., go about some of her old duties, happy to have something to do. Now, however, any of that former socializing with her peers was out of the question, and the whispers about Effie's status as a full-time resident of the hotel had grown to outright gossip. Whenever Effie traveled inside the hotel---and she was told never to leave---she felt that her old friends and co-workers were talking behind her back, disapprovingly commenting on her expanding form, passing judgment on her behavior. She could not visit her parents or siblings and—good Baptist folk that they were---they would not visit her in R.B.'s Taj Mahal. They were ashamed that their unmarried daughter was big with child, and they had forbidden even her sympathetic siblings to offer any encouragement or support to Effie by visiting.

Although the talk of R.B.'s illegitimate child was now quite widespread in certain circles, R.B. made it clear to Effie that she must stay in the penthouse, in order to keep their relationship and their child a secret from his three children by his former wife. Ruby was already leading the charge on removing Robert B. Sherman from control of the fortune he had acquired. What would Ruby do if she were to find out about Effie and the baby?

"But…R.B.….the baby is walking now. Little Effie's never even been outside. She deserves to feel the sun on her face. Maybe she even deserves to get to know her half-sisters and half-brother? Sooner or later, she must go to school."

When R.B. heard these ideas, which he termed "crazy talk," he instantly secured security guards to constantly stand guard outside the penthouse doors. The guards made sure that Effie Waterman didn't wander off or reveal the secret the couple had agreed to share. Effie was now virtually a prisoner within the walls of the Sherman Hotel.

"Now, honey. You know we can't have Ruby and Maggie and Robert, Jr., gettin' all riled up about you and the baby?"

"Why not? What's wrong with me? What's wrong with Little Effie? Don't you love us? Are you ashamed of us?"

"Of course I love you, darlin', but it wouldn't do to give Ruby and Maggie and Robert, Junior, any ammunition to fight me with. They don't want me to expand the hotel again. This time, I want to build a new tower across Broadway. Ruby doesn't want me to and she's convinced Maggie and Robert, Junior, to oppose me, too. Ruby wants me to keep drillin' for oil in Oklahoma." R.B. paused to light another cigar and a far-away look lit up his pale blue eyes. "Ah! You'll see. The hotel'll be grand and you'll have the catbird's seat…a bird's-eye view from the Penthouse. It's going to be a 28-story tower. This will be the best damned hotel in all of the Midwest. Hell! It'll be the best damned hotel in the whole United States of

America! And you'll be part of it, because, you see, I want you to stay here, in the hotel, with me. You're livin' in the lap of luxury. The top floor penthouse of the best hotel in the country? Do you want for anything? Aren't you well fed? Aren't you well housed? Aren't you treated well? Doesn't the baby have everything she needs?"

"But I'm lonely, R.B......"

"Lonely! Pshaw! That's no big deal. You know I'll come visit you."
"Yes, you'll come, but I don't get to go out. I don't get to see my mother, my father, my brothers and sisters, my friends. I don't ever get to leave. The baby never gets to leave."

"Darling, you're just a little unhinged about having a baby. That's all. It happens to women all the time, especially women as young as you." R.B.'s withered hand stroked her pink youthful cheek.

"No, R.B. Little Effie is almost a year old, and I haven't been allowed to leave the penthouse in all that time." Effie repeated this complaint whenever R.B visited. It soon poisoned the time they spent together, and R.B. began to spend more and more time at his club, smoking his beloved

Cuban cigars and kibbitzing with his cronies, instead of visiting Effie and his new daughter. This only made Effie grow more and more despondent. The familiar refrain played out over and over during R.B. Skirvin's clandestine visits to Effie, until, one day, he forbade her to speak of it to him ever again.

"Honey, you know you can't go gallivanting around just now. Ruby and Maggie and Robert are fighting me for control. If they find out about you…"

R.B. left the rest of the statement unfinished, but his silence was eloquent. The next day, the crushed and bloody bodies of a woman and child, Effie and Little Effie, were found on the sidewalk beneath the Sherman Hotel Penthouse balcony. It appeared that the distraught mother had clutched her child to her bosom and leaped from the exterior balcony of the hotel, although it was never clear at what dim dark hour of the dawn the catastrophe might have occurred. There were even those who whispered of foul play, but nothing ever appeared in any Chelsea newspapers about the deaths of mother and child. There was no investigation. There was a very private cremation service. There was no burial plot. There were no grave markers to mark the place where Effie Waterman and her child lay.

Legal battles continued to strain Sherman family relations in 1949, when Ruby Miller, R..B.'s daughter, who had married wealthy businessman George Miller, filed a lawsuit in the 10th. U.S. Circuit Court of Appeals, trying to oust her father from the management of the hotel and from running his own affairs.

   Maggie, the younger daughter, had also returned home by that point in time, after dropping a career as a stage and screen actress. Maggie married Robert Miller and returned to live in the Sherman Hotel for several years with her daughter, Beatrice. It was Maggie's presence in the hotel that had made R.B. especially careful not to let Effie or Little Effie fly away from the love nest he had made for her. It was Maggie's roaming of the hallways with her own child that had precipitated the hiring of the guards who insisted that Effie never leave her penthouse love nest. (Except, it seems, by the window).

On March 11, 1944, the 10th U.S. Circuit judge ruled that R.B. Sherman, then 80 years old, was as mentally sharp as ever, and completely competent to manage his 300-room hotel, if he wished to do so, which quelled the mutiny of R.B.'s legitimate heirs. After all, said the judge in defending R..B. against charges of mis-management that led to hotel losses, the entire economy was depressed throughout the 1930s, not just the state of Oklahoma and the Sherman Hotel.

The judge also said, "You Shermans ought to be ashamed of yourselves! This lawsuit has been like Sherman's March to the Sea: bringing death and destruction to everyone in its path and serving no useful purpose, in the long run." Whether the Judge was privately referencing Effie's death is not known. R.B. Sherman was too powerful a man to publicly go against. He had had more than one judge removed from his post in his day.

The local press buried the story of the mother and child's fall from the Sherman Hotel's highest balcony. No mention. No story. No coverage of the disposal of the bodies.

Perhaps the judge found the fight over R.B. Sherman's assets, while R..B. was still alive and well, unseemly. The judge said, in ruling for R..B. and against Ruby and her brother and sister, "Age alone of an owner or manager of a property is not enough to warrant the appointment of a receiver or the continuation of an existing receivership. R.B. Skirvin is 80 years of age and if the properties are restored by their owners, he may again become the active manager until such time as evidence, not just animosity, can prove his incompetence."

As R.B. Skirvin lay dying...consumed by guilt over his dead mistress and their child,....R..B. said, to his three surviving children, "I've forgiven you. There's nothing but love in my heart for all three of you children; you're all I have."

R.B. might have added, "You're the only children I have *now*. Now that Effie and Little Effie are dead."

Ever since the day of Effie's death, guests at the hotel have seen maids' carts move mysteriously down the hall, no human in sight. Guests hear voices: the crying of a woman and a child. One male guest said he heard a woman outside his bathroom shower door saying, "Can I come in and be with you? I'm so lonely. Can I join you, please?" The guest was afraid to come out of the shower!

Guests of the Sherman Hotel continued to hear the mysterious crying of a woman and a child after Effie's death until the hotel, itself, closed in 1988. There were continued reports of maids' carts moving mysteriously in the hallways, unattended by live maids...especially on the fourteenth floor. Men would sometimes see a naked woman in their shower or hear a soft female voice crying, whimpering, begging for company. Small children heard the voice of a little girl crying inconsolably.

The strains of the fabled parties of Ruby Sherman in the nation's Capitol have long since given way to cries of despair and betrayal from Effie and her daughter. May they rest in peace.

*This is the end of the journey, the end of Route 66. We'll continue our travels soon...*

BOOKS BY MICHAEL McCARTY:

Nonfiction:

*Giants of the Genre*  (2003, Wildside Press)
*More Giants of the Genre*  (2005, Wildside Press)
*Ghosts of Route 66 (Book One),* co-written with Connie Corcoran Wilson (2007, Quixote Press)
*Modern Mythmakers*  (McFarland & Company, 2008)

Short Story Collections:

*Dark Duets*  (2005, Wildside Press)
*All Things Dark And Hideous,* co-written with Mark McLaughlin (Rainfall Books, England, 2008)
*Little Creatures* (Sam's Dot Publishing, 2008)

Novel:

*Monster Behind The Wheel,* co-written with Mark McLaughlin (Corrosion Press/Delirium Books, 2008)
*Liquid Diet* (Demonic Clown/Black Death Books, 2008)

Novella:

*Monster Hunter* (Skullvines Press, 2008)

BOOKS BY CONNIE CORCORAN WILSON:

Nonfiction:

*Training the Teacher As A Champion* (co-author) (Performance Learning Systems, 1989)

*Ghosts of Route 66 (Book One),* co-written with Michael McCarty (2007, Quixote Press)

Short Story & Poetry Collection:

*Both Sides Now* (1st Books Library, 2003)

## MICHAEL McCARTY:

Michael McCarty is a former stand-up comedian, musician and managing editor of a music magazine. His first book *Giants Of The Genre* (Wildside Press 2003) was a collection of interviews with the greats of science fiction, horror and fantasy. His second book, *More Giants Of The Genre*, featured twenty-five new interviews and was a Bram Stoker Finalist for Nonfiction book of the Year (Wildside Press, 2005). He also wrote the short story collection entitled *Dark Duets* (Wildside Press 2005). His first novel, a collaboration with Bram Stoker winner Mark McLaughlin, *Monster Behind the Wheel* will be published in Corrosion Press/Delirium Books in July 2008 and his first novella *Monster Hunter* will come out sometime in 2009 from Skullvines Press. His second short story collection, also co-written with Mark McLaughlin, *All Things Dark and Hideous,* was published in England in the fall of 2007 by Rainfall Books. The nonfiction book of ghost stories *Ghosts of Route 66* (co-written with Connie Corcoran Wilson) was published by Quixote Press. He is a staff writer for "Science Fiction Weekly" (the website of the Sci Fi Channel). Michael graduated from Marycrest College with a B.A. in both English and Journalism. He can be reached at mikelmccarty@hotmail.com or P.O. Box 4441, Rock Island, IL 61201. His websites are:
www.geocities.com/mccartyzone,
www.myspace.com/route66ghosts and
www.myspace.com/monsterbook.

## CONNIE CORCORAN WILSON:

Connie is a graduate of the University of Iowa, with a Master's degree from Western Illinois University and 30 additional graduate hours in English and Journalism from Berkeley, Northern Illinois University, Western Illinois University, University of Iowa and the University of Chicago. She has taught composition at six colleges and written for five newspapers. For twelve years, Connie was the film and book critic for the *Quad City Times* (Davenport, Iowa). She also conducted celebrity interviews for the Moline, Illinois *Daily Dispatch* and wrote a weekly humor column for newspapers in East Moline and Rock Island, Illinois.

Her first book, *Training the Teacher As A Champion,* was published in 1989 by Performance Learning Systems, Inc.

After teaching junior high school language arts at Silvis Junior High School from 1969 until 1985, Connie established the Sylvan Learning Center in Bettendorf, Iowa, the second in the state in Iowa in 1986. In 1995, she added the Prometric Testing Center. She served as CEO of both businesses until 2002.

In 2003 she published *Both Sides Now*, a book of previously published humor columns and poetry.

In 2007 she co-authored *Ghosts of Route 66 (Book One)* with Michael McCarty.

Connie is married to Craig, and has a son and daughter (Scott and Stacey). Her website are:
www.ConnieCorcoranWilson.com
www.myspace.com/conniecorcoranwilson
www.myspace.com/route66ghosts

## To Order Copies

Please send me _____ copies of ***Ghosts of Route 66*** at $9.95 each plus $3.00 S/H. (Make checks payable to Quixote Press.)

Name _____

Street _____

City _____ State _____ Zip _____

**QUIXOTE PRESS**
**3544 Blakslee Street**
**Wever IA 52658**
**1-800-571-2665**

---

## To Order Copies

Please send me _____ copies of ***Ghosts of Route 66*** at $9.95 each plus $3.00 S/H. (Make checks payable to Quixote Press.)

Name _____

Street _____

City _____ State _____ Zip _____

**QUIXOTE PRESS**
**3544 Blakslee Street**
**Wever IA 52658**
**1-800-571-2665**

| |
|---|
| **GHOSTS OF INTERSTATE 90** Chicago to Boston    by D. Latham |
| *GHOSTS of the Whitewater Valley* by Chuck Grimes |
| **GHOSTS of Interstate 74**    by B. Carlson |
| GHOSTS of the Ohio Lakeshore Counties    by Karen Waltemire |
| *GHOSTS of Interstate 65* by Joanna Foreman |
| **GHOSTS of Interstate 25** by Bruce Carlson |
| **GHOSTS of the Smoky Mountains** by Larry Hillhouse |
| GHOSTS of the Illinois Canal System    by David Youngquist |
| *GHOSTS of the Niagara River*    by Bruce Carlson |
| **Ghosts of Little Bavaria**    by Kishe Wallace |
| Ghosts of Des Moines County    by Bruce Carlson |

Shown above (at 85% of actual size) are the spines of other Quixote Press books of ghost stories. These are available at the retailer from whom this book was procured, or from our office at 1-800-571-2665 cost is $9.95 + $3.50 S/H.

*Ghosts of Lake Erie* — by Jo Lela Pope Kimber

**GHOSTS OF DALLAS COUNTY** — by Lori Pielak

**Ghosts of US - 66** — by Michael McCarty & Connie Corcoran Wilson

Ghosts of the Appalachian Trail — by Dr. Tirstan Perry

**Ghosts of I-70** — by B. Carlson

Ghosts of the Thousand Islands — by Larry Hillhouse

*Ghosts of US - 23 in Michigan* — by B. Carlson

**Ghosts of Lake Superior** — by Enid Cleaves

***GHOSTS OF THE IOWA GREAT LAKES*** — by Bruce Carlson

*Ghosts of the Amana Colonies* — by Lori Erickson

**Ghosts of Lee County, Iowa** — by Bruce Carlson

The Best of the Mississippi River Ghosts — by Bruce Carlson

**Ghosts of Polk County Iowa** — by Tom Welch

| | |
|---|---|
| **GHOSTS of Lookout Mountain** | by Larry Hillhouse |
| *GHOSTS of Interstate 77* | by Bruce Carlson |
| **GHOSTS of Interstate 94** | by B. Carlson |
| **GHOSTS of MICHIGAN'S U. P.** | by Chris Shanley-Dillman |
| GHOSTS of the FOX RIVER VALLEY | by D. Latham |
| *GHOSTS ALONG I-35* | *by B. Carlson* |
| **Ghosts of Lake Huron** | **by Roger H. Meyer** |
| Ghost Stories by Kids, for Kids | by some really great fifth graders |
| Ghosts of Door County Wisconsin | by Geri Rider |
| *Ghosts of the Ozarks* | *B Carlson* |
| **Ghosts of US - 63** | by Bruce Carlson |